Deals In Blood

A FANTASY ANTHOLOGY

DEALS IN BLOOD

First edition.
Copyright © A. A. Warne 2023

Cover: Yukimi Lumaris
Editor: Amy Elmore
Topography: Bruno Gomes
Format: A. A. Warne

This is a work of fiction. Any similarity between characters and situations within its pages and places or persons, living or dead, is unintentional and coincidental.

Foreword

You know how you can meet people and then they're a permanent fixture in your life? That's what happened to me in January 2017. I signed up for a MasterClass, hoping to better myself as a writer. I came away with a friend for life. For six years, I've witnessed A. A. Warne grow as a writer, branch out into publishing, and build her platform. She's stubborn, tenacious, wildly creative, and the captain of this fantastical ship you're about to set sail on. Each of the writers in this collection was selected by her, but her influence didn't stop there. Through coaching, advocating, securing badass beta readers (I was fortunate to make this list), and a fantastic editor (Amy), A. A. Warne helped each of the writers elevate their stories to the page-turners you're about to read.

This collection consists of dark fantasy stories, where deals made in blood and magic always come with a hefty price. Some characters are more willing than others to carry that weight to reach their deepest, most sinister desires. You'll meet a feline humanoid bred for entertainment and bound for a life of slavery, who claws their way to freedom. You'll see that sometimes, despite best intentions and a bit of dark magic, love just isn't enough. You'll witness the devastation of a future royal line and the budding of a sinister monster in its wake. There's more in this collection but I'll stop there and let you read for yourself.

Like all creative pieces, these short stories are finely crafted by their authors. The characters niggling at their brains— appeased only once their stories are made flesh. These are stories that beg to be read at night, alone, in the dark.

- *Michelle Crow*

Shootout at Shenashani

RALPH RORICKSON

F arrow shouldered the cabin door open, hauling a heavy burlap sack over his shoulder. His whole body ached, twigs and tree bark mussed his shaggy, dark-red hair, and his wide-brimmed hat sat askew on his head, yet his heart was high. That sack contained one of the last few keys needed to unlock his freedom.

He called out, "Got the hair."

A single large, dingy room made up the cabin's interior, filled with many shelves and cupboards laden with old tomes, notebooks, and dusty glass containers; a large cauldron that was in better condition than anything else; and a messy desk. Hunched over the desk, writing in a notebook by the light of a dim oil lamp, sat a hooded figure.

"Set it by the cauldron," the figure said, its masculine voice like dry paper crumpling.

Farrow dropped the sack with a thump where instructed, then slipped the revolver on his hip from its holster and checked the cylinder. Two shots left. "Got any more bullets?"

The figure kept writing, pen rasping against paper.

"Nemo?"

Finally, the lich looked up. Under his cowl glowered a withered gray face with desiccated lips pulled back over unnaturally white teeth. Large, gleaming gemstones filled his eye sockets. "Where's the rifle?"

"Damned agropelter broke it." Farrow had been tasked with killing the beast for its hair. It had only been by a lucky shot through its eye that he'd managed to do so with the handgun.

Nemo turned back to his book. "You won't need the bullets."

"I *want* 'em," he insisted.

The lich pointed a gnarled gray finger to a bottom shelf. "There."

"Yeah, thanks." Farrow searched the shelf, his eyes unhindered by the dark, and found a box full of bullets. Sighing, he removed his hat. A pair of feline ears twitched atop his head.

It had been almost two years since Nemokeros first found Farrow. Farrow had been fleeing through the forested hills for three days. The main thing he recalled from that time was being numb from the cold nights and rainy days, and having so many bug bites he forgot what it was like to not itch. He ached from running with nothing in his belly but leaves and water from the few drinkable streams he happened upon.

Eventually, fatigue overtook him, and he collapsed by the edge of a small, stagnant pond. When he opened his eyes, he found Nemo's decrepit face staring down at him, framed by a faded hood and the gray mist of morning.

Farrow's throat tightened. "Am I dead?"

"No," Nemo replied, "but I think you will be soon."

Farrow choked on a weak sob.

The lich cocked his head. "You're a biform."

"Y-ye . . ." Farrow swallowed hard. "Yes." His mix of

human and feline features—the ears, a long tail, fanged incisors, even his sharp hooked nails—wasn't natural. He'd been *made*, the result of combining human and animal life energies. Brewed like a cheap drink.

Nemo spotted the brand burned into his right shoulder, an owl in flight over a six-pointed star. "Made to a particular specification, I take it."

Farrow nodded, voice too tight to speak. His lithe build, wavy hair, and green-gold eyes had also been designed.

"Some of the most sophisticated spellcraft ever conceived," Nemo muttered, "and some idiots are using it to make pets." He looked over at something to his right. "No offense."

Farrow winced.

"I can save you," said the lich, turning back to Farrow. "But you'll have to repay me."

Farrow tensed. "How?"

"I need assistance. Fetching supplies, equipment, and so on." He pointed to his right. There sat a basket full of various mushrooms and leaves. "I will save you, and you will assist me in collecting what I need until the debt is paid. One year of service."

The reek of cold, musty decay surrounded Nemo, like an animal frozen to death in the deep winter. Farrow considered taking his chances alone. But as he was—shivering, starving, chewed apart by bugs—what were his odds? At best, he might crawl a bit farther before he wasted away. At worst, *they* would catch up with him and take him back.

He said, "I accept."

Nemo reached for his hand. "I'll need your blood." When Farrow gasped and tore his hand away, the lich added, "Only a little to ensure you can't back out before your debt is paid. It's part of the deal."

Farrow clenched his jaw, glaring back into those white

stone eyes. But again, what choice did he have? He gave his hand. The lich drew a small syringe from within his cloak, then rolled down Farrow's sleeve and pricked the needle into his forearm.

Now, Farrow slotted the last bullet into the revolver's cylinder and clapped it back into the frame. Nemo had kept his word. He'd brought the lost biform back to his cabin, got him fed, warm, and patched up. Then he'd taught Farrow the skills he would need, given him a detailed list of what he required and how to find it, and sent him back into the forest.

The deal hadn't been bad. The work was dirty and rough, but Farrow found it satisfying. Before, he had been an accessory, born to sit in a gilded cage and look pretty. Now he dug for roots and bland bugs, and even scraped fungus from logs. It wasn't an ideal life either, but it felt good to be valued for what he could *do* with his own sweat and muscle rather than what he'd been made to look like. Not a pet.

Nemo hobbled over to the sack and dragged it to a wooden chest. "Go rest."

Farrow holstered the revolver and slipped out into the cool night air, retiring to a small shack set aside for him nearby. It held little more than a chest for his clothes, a rickety bed, a small fireplace, and a coldbox dug into the dirt. Within the coldbox was half a loaf of hard bread, several apples, and some deer jerky, all kept edible by a gem infused with cold magic.

He tidied up his hair with a brush from the chest, the only trinket he'd kept from his old life. When Farrow had escaped his prison, he'd brought the brush along on impulse. Later, he wrestled with whether or not to keep it, torn between the simple comfort it brought him, the peaceful rhythm of brushing out his curls, and the memories of humiliation and captivity. Sometimes, he swore he could still feel the too-tight collar he'd been forced to wear digging into his throat. Sometimes, his claws still ached from the file used to dull them after he had lashed out at someone who couldn't keep their hands to themselves.

The memory raked through Farrow's mind like a cold wind. That had been the only time he'd stood up for himself. Afterward, he'd been rewarded by being propped up in a wooden chair. A spell was used to stiffen his body so he had to sit there, paralyzed for the next several hours. The amber flame of a lantern flickered no more than a foot from his face. Holding it and towering over him stood a tall, rigid crow of a woman, the fine emerald dress and layers of makeup she wore meant to distract from the sharp edges of her wrinkled face. Everything about her was an act, right down to the title she gave herself: Madam.

"What have I told you, Farrow?" Madam scolded in her thin, croaking voice which pierced his ears. She crossed her arms, posture so straight and rigid one might think she was tied to a post herself. "You are meant to make our guests feel *invited.*"

Farrow could not respond. Even his eyelids had been frozen open. His eyes stung from the water that dripped into them every so often. He wanted to ask, *If I'm not supposed to use my claws, why'd you give them to me?*

"Ms. Eckarsatt is an important patron at our establishment," continued Madam, "and I paid a lot to have you made. All I ask is that you make that investment pay off."

Madam looked down her nose at his claws. Fresh blood stained their tips. She barked, "Hackens!"

A broad, hairy boar of a man stood against the back wall of the small room, his greasy hair tied back into a ponytail to give him a thin veneer of gentility. He stepped forward. "Ma'am."

Madam moved aside. "Ensure that Farrow can't cause any further trouble."

Hackens approached, a mix of amusement and morbid fascination in his small, blue eyes. "Yes, ma'am." From the pocket of his red vest, he pulled a nail file.

Farrow shook the recollection off. He was away from that place now. *I'm never going back.*

Besides, it was a nice enough brush, and after some consideration, he'd decided that he didn't mind looking presentable—he just didn't want that to be all he was worth. He refused to let the memories ruin that for him, refused to let *her* retain any kind of control over him. And after all, the brush would be handy in his life to come.

He replaced that dark memory with a more hopeful one. "You can make me human," he'd once asked Nemo, "right?"

Nemo looked up from the heap of joint snake scales on his desk, which Farrow had delivered to him earlier that day.

"I mean . . ." Farrow didn't fully understand the process that had created him, but he knew it was based on mixing the magical energies of different living things together. "You can just take the cat out, and I'll be a full human, right?"

"It won't be that simple," replied Nemo. "But theoretically, yes."

Farrow wiped a patch of icy mud from his jawline. "Can you or can't you?"

"I can." Nemo brushed the scales into a leather purse. "It won't be pleasant, though."

"That's fine." Farrow was already well acquainted with unpleasantness.

"I'll need supplies to do it, and you'll need to repay me again. Another year of service."

Farrow nodded. "That's fine, too." If he were human, he wouldn't need to hide anymore. His life could finally and fully be his own. For that, he'd dig and scrape around in these woods for a decade.

Nemo had tied the purse shut and hobbled over to place it on a shelf. "Then it's a deal."

Farrow woke at dawn to four hard knocks on his door.

"I need something," said Nemo from outside.

Farrow crawled out from under the covers. "What is it?" The bread and jerky he'd eaten last night still sat heavy in his stomach. A nervous, giddy anticipation had kept him awake for some time. The two years were almost up.

"Ectoplasm. One vial."

Farrow rubbed his eyes. "Where am I going to find that?"

"Shenashani River," croaked Nemo. "Plenty of restless dead there."

It took Farrow a moment to recognize the name. "Oh."

Shenashani River had been the site of a major battle in the war, around fifteen years ago. Farrow hadn't the faintest idea what the fighting had been about. He'd been a kid, hidden away from the world in his gilded cage, but everyone knew that a lot of people had died, particularly along the Shenashani.

"Don't forget the syringe," Nemo added before he left with the clicking of old joints and a rustle of dirty fabric.

Farrow rubbed the sleep from his eyes. He didn't look forward to dealing with ghosts, but he was nearly free. Never mind the revolver; he'd wrestle an agropelter with his bare hands for that.

He ate a light breakfast of bread and berries, bathed quickly in the nearby pond, then packed a satchel and dressed. Slipping into Nemo's cabin, he grabbed a large syringe with a needle made of lustrous silver metal from a cabinet and left.

Shenashani River was a day's walk northeast. Farrow had come to know the forest well, however, and had discovered some shortcuts. His feline attributes allowed him to move quickly and quietly through the underbrush, his eyes adapted to the dark and his ears able to pick up the faintest sounds. That would get him there just before dusk.

The cat part of him had its uses, he admitted to himself. He'd even once considered staying a biform, but his kind was rare, and most folks knew biforms weren't natural. Even setting aside how unusual he'd be, someone might recognize him. Madam would have an easier time finding him as well, so if he wanted to live free, he needed to be as human as possible.

Fingers of amber evening light beckoned him through the trees as the daylight started to recede. Farrow heard the rumbling river as he emerged onto the rocky bank of the Shenashani, his face caressed by the fine mist rising from the dark, rushing water. The river cut through the land, spanning almost a hundred feet wide. Here and there, still half-buried amid the mud and stone of the bank, lay an old musket or saber, or even a rusted iron post used to protect against enemy magic. On both sides of the water, some of the trees were missing chunks that had been blown out of their sides by cannon fire, and several smaller ones had been knocked down. Farrow had no attachment to the war or the men who'd fought it, but even so, he shivered.

A short distance down the bank, Farrow found the stone bridge spanning the river. From what he knew of ghosts, they became more active at sundown. All he had to do then was poke one with the syringe to retrieve the ectoplasm. If all went well, his biggest concern would be making sure no wolves or cougars snuck up on him. He made his way onto the bridge, then sat down against the railing at the halfway point and waited.

Daylight faded and night replaced it. All became silent, save for the odd hoot of an owl in the forest. Once, Farrow heard what sounded like a shout deeper in the woods, but he took it for fur trappers since there was a trading post not far from Nemo's cabin. Dark clouds rolled above but couldn't quite cover the full moon. Farrow buttoned up his jacket against the cold. Then he slipped one hand into his pocket to feel for the syringe and braced himself.

Through the trees came more voices, dull and echoing as if heard underwater. After that, many soft pops erupted along both shores of the river, followed by muffled screams. A chill brushed over the fine hair covering Farrow's body. It was time. He rose to a crouch and peered over the railing.

Mist had settled along the banks of the river; through it, he could see soldiers standing in firing formation. Those on the south shore wore dull-green uniforms, while those on the north were dressed in brown with black caps. The soldiers on either side numbered in the hundreds, although some had been struck down by the first volley of musket fire. Several of these lay still, but many more writhed and cried out as some of their comrades hurried out of the trees to pull them to safety. Farrow spotted gaps in the lines, places where men should have been but weren't. The soldiers who had stood there must have survived the war, or at least the Battle of Shenashani itself.

Farrow picked one of the ghosts who lay still on the south shore and hurried over. As he approached, he saw that the figures shimmered ever so slightly, like mirages in the desert. The men they resembled were dead, and these ghosts were merely their echoes, imprinted upon this place by the vast amounts of life magic that had been released so suddenly and violently. Over time, they would fade more and more until they disappeared altogether, but they were still fresh enough now.

As he crept through the crowd of phantoms, Farrow tried not to focus on their faces or voices. It seemed cruel to him that the echoes of their deaths bound them here. Even after their lives had ended, they were still trapped in the war.

The world's just damned mean, isn't it?

Many, he couldn't help but notice, were boys as young as he, perhaps even younger. Their huge, frightened eyes stared over their muskets. He passed a man who was shouting something from behind the front line. The wrinkles around his wide eyes looked like they'd been carved there with a knife. Swallowing, Farrow tore his gaze away.

At last, Farrow reached his mark and knelt down by the fallen phantom. Taking the syringe from his pocket, he poked the needle into its chest. The surface resisted briefly, then quivered like pudding as the needle slipped in. He swallowed an urge to retch and drew the plunger back. Slowly, the needle filled with a dull gray-green sludge. Once the syringe was full, he pulled it back out.

Before Farrow could put the syringe away, something crackled past his ears. A flash of pale light filled his vision, then struck the river's surface and dissipated.

What in every hell? He flinched, then stole a look into the trees. Through the swarm of shadows, three solid figures approached, the tails of their long, dark coats shifting like wings as they crept forward. In their hands were wands, the tips glowing with misty silver light.

Farrow darted back to the bridge as more bolts of light snapped past him. Once again, his feline reflexes and agility aided him. Ducking under the railing, he scurried across the river.

From the opposite shore, a familiar voice bellowed, "Come out, boy. This don't have to get ugly." Hackens.

Farrow gritted his teeth. They'd finally tracked him down. But after two years, of course they had. *I should have run farther. I should have stayed with Nemo for only one year. I should have . . .*

Trembling with rage and fear, he reached the end of the bridge and broke for the forest. A trio of silver shots peppered the brush ahead of him. They must be stunning spells, he realized. Desperate, he dove into the thick of the ghosts, hoping to hide in their midst, and scrambled toward the tree line.

Farrow blinked back hot, angry tears as spectral bodies slipped around him. He dared to glance back over his shoulder. All he saw at first, however, were the battle lines of the ghosts on the opposite shore. Only occasionally did he glimpse the darker shapes of his attackers as they darted in between the phantoms toward the bridge.

"Come back with us," Hackens shouted. "It's only gonna hurt if you fight."

"Don't you wanna go back?" called another man. "You'll catch your death out here. Or fleas."

"You're worth more without bruises," said the third, "but Madam'll take you either way."

Worth. Farrow swallowed hard. That was all his life had ever been about. His hands curled into fists, clenched so hard his unfiled claws dug into his palms. Who were they to decide his worth? When did he get to decide his own? If they had wanted him to be an obedient little animal, they shouldn't have given him a man's mind.

Closer now, boots scuffed on stone. But Farrow had finally reached the forest. Scrambling behind a tree, he paused to breathe. He had to fight. It was that, or go back to the cage. He set his mouth into a hard line. The choice was obvious.

Grabbing the revolver from his hip, he pulled the hammer back. *Now, I decide.*

The second man taunted, "We'll catch you some nice fish on the way back, don't you worry."

Their bootsteps drew closer and closer. When they were almost across the bridge, Farrow peeked out from behind the thick trunk. The trio crept along, keeping a low profile so only their hats were visible above the railing. He waited for the first to step out from behind it. Once the dark figure stalked into sight, he took aim, holding his breath to steady his hand. Then he squeezed the trigger.

The gunshot rang in his ears, and the man fell back onto the bridge, grabbing his throat with an awful, wet gurgle. Farrow darted back into cover, teeth bared in grim satisfaction as he pulled the hammer back.

"Dammit," grunted Hackens as something heavy was dragged across stone. A spell screamed through the brush past Farrow.

After that came a still moment. Farrow's ears caught whispers. Between the echoes of the phantom battle and the roar of the river, he couldn't make out the words. Trembling from a cocktail of adrenaline, fury, and dread, he peered out again.

The last two hunters rushed out, one breaking right and the other left. Both disappeared into the crowds of ghosts, where Farrow almost lost them. As they got closer, however, they became easier to see. Taking aim at the one on the right, he squinted. If not for his feline eyes, the dark might have obscured the man, but the night couldn't hide anything from him.

A ghost stepped into the hunter's path, and he charged right through it. Its image rippled, and the living man stumbled as the semi-liquid mass resisted him. Farrow took his shot. The hunter grunted and spun around as it hit him in the shoulder. Farrow fired again. With a spasm, the hunter collapsed.

A gun cracked, and a bullet—not a spell—whizzed past Farrow's head. "You little shit," snarled Hackens, charging his way with a rifle drawn. "I'll skin you alive!"

Scrambling around the tree trunk for cover, Farrow tried to come up with a plan, but adrenaline and desperation fogged his thoughts.

I'm not going back. The mantra reverberated in his mind. Anything would be better than going back.

"To hell with it." The hunter trudged through the brush toward Farrow. "If you die, you die. Madam can just make another. You ain't worth all this."

Farrow's ears flattened into his hair. He checked the revolver's cylinder. Three bullets left. With the enemy so near, there was no time to reload. Mind racing, he stood up.

The hunter's footsteps slowed as he approached, twigs and leaves crinkling under his boots. Farrow's heart hammered against his breastbone as if to break out.

Hackens paused when he was a few yards away. Then he started left around the trunk. Farrow slipped around the right side and fired at his back.

Hackens lunged behind the tree to evade. Leaping out beside Farrow, he charged the biform, a grimace in the depths of his grimy black beard. But Farrow was fast, too. As the hunter swung the butt of the rifle at his head, Farrow ducked and darted away.

"Get back here!" Hackens' voice sounded like rumbling stone. He fired a potshot after Farrow, and the biform threw himself behind another tree. The hunter's heavy feet thumped after him.

Dammit, he's right on me. Farrow could keep running, sure. He was still faster. Maybe he could even get away with the vial of ectoplasm, but Hackens would still be after him. This had to end. In fact, he intended to end it this very night. He regained his feet, dug his claws into the bark, and began to climb.

Farrow did not climb often. His arms soon throbbed with the strain as he pulled himself higher and higher. Hackens stalked closer, growling under his breath. Farrow gritted his teeth and kept going.

Soon, the hunter was almost under him. Storming around the trunk, Hackens stopped, huffing. Farrow dared to peer down and saw the hunter's greasy head whipping from side to side.

"Where'd you go, boy?"

Despite himself, Farrow smirked. Then he pulled his claws free of the bark and dropped onto Hackens' back.

There was a distinct size difference between them. Hackens had been hired for his solid build, whereas Farrow had been made lithe and slender to accentuate his feline nature. Hackens barely flinched when the biform landed on his shoulders, which was why Farrow fought dirty. Vising his legs around Hackens' neck, he went for the hunter's eyes first, raking claws deep into his face.

Hackens screamed and tried to pry him off. Farrow latched on harder, digging his nails into his foe's matted beard with one hand while the other shredded his face like old cloth.

I'm not going back.

Hackens buckled, the rifle slipping from his grip. Then he seized Farrow by the knees, his fingers like barbs of cold iron. With a gurgling roar of effort, he dragged Farrow's legs apart, then spun around and hurled him down the slope.

Farrow grabbed at the soil in an attempt to stop himself, but his head swam as he rolled. He struck bushes and small stones, each one knocking the sense from him bit by bit. By the time he came to a stop on the riverbank, all he felt was pain. He blinked and gasped, trying to rise.

"*Little freak bastard!*" Hackens roared from above.

Farrow fought to regain his feet. Fallen men lay in a carpet all around him. The ghosts who still moved now skirmished on the bridge, hacking and stabbing with bayonets and sabers.

A bullet splashed into the river. Farrow spun around to see Hackens staggering toward him. The man's face was a dark-red ruin, only the stark white of his teeth visible as he sneered. He tottered about, sweeping his rifle across the shore.

He can't see.

"Think I won't find you?" the hunter seethed. "I know you're here, boy."

Farrow inhaled to steady his hand and took aim. The hunter wiped the blood from his eyes and blinked just in time to see the revolver pointed at him. His eyes widened.

Farrow fired. Hackens' head snapped back, and he collapsed onto the dirt.

A moment passed as Farrow listened and watched the body. The dull clamor of the phantom battle echoed around him, but Hackens didn't move. The biform hastily reloaded, looking around just in case. By the time that was done, he still found himself alone.

He dug the syringe out of the felled soldier and inspected it for damage. The cylinder was still full of ectoplasm. A tremor ran through him.

I think that's it.

Could that really be it? Once he took this back to Nemo, would that really be all? He'd be free? Clutching the syringe to his chest, Farrow swallowed hard. After so long in cages, after two years of hard work, he would be *free*. It seemed too good to be true. He could have wept at the thought.

Instead, he blinked back the tears and smiled. Tucking the syringe into his satchel, he made his way across the bridge. The ghosts still fought around him, and he walked through several of them, a sensation like passing through a dense, cold fog.

On the other side, his freedom awaited.

About the Author

Hailing from northern Canada, Ralph Rorickson grew up on sci-fi, fantasy, and adventure stories of all mediums. While he always had a passion to share his own stories in this genre, he didn't settle on writing until high school, and went on to get his bachelor's in creative writing. He self-published his debut fantasy novel, Onyx Crown, Book One: Driftwood Empire, at the start of 2022, and is currently working on the sequel with plans to release in late 2023.

Website: https://ko-fi.com/ralphrorricksonauthor

The Hemologist

M J J MORI

"Welcome!" said the aged shopkeeper, his long beard twitching as he spoke. "Yes, please enter. Don't just stand there lurking in the doorway, halfway between this world and the next."

The hooded customer quietly entered the timeworn store and glanced around the crooked shelves overflowing with dusty vials. "I was told there are blood solutions here?" he inquired, stepping into a shadowed corner.

The shopkeeper drew himself up in his fraying robes and announced, "You have stepped into a house of high repute! I am Yarin Yarr, purveyor of organic enchantments and supplier to kings and queens." He grandly waved his arms around the multitude of variously sized crystal vials, each with a tiny label attached. "I deal in only the finest of corpuscular liquids. Indeed, you have heard correctly: we specialize in bloods"—he pointed to different areas of the room as he spoke—"of every type: of beast and bird, of insect and crustacea, of predator and prey."

The customer mumbled and turned toward the shelves.

"Pardon me? You're only browsing? Of course, of course, don't let me interrupt you." Yarr paused for a brief moment before continuing his pitch. "Each vial lining these shelves is clearly labeled with the source, date, and age of extraction." He took his potential client's arm and led the man to a certain shelf. "If you please, allow me to recommend beginning in the mammalian section. Mostly familiar items here, no? Cow, sheep, pig. Horse, dog, cat. Goat, lamb, maiden. Yes, all very common." He lowered his voice. "Look closely, though. Some of the vials you'll find are of a rare species. Even a handful of the ones I have are increasingly difficult to obtain. Impossible, you might say."

"Any ill-gotten elements?" asked the customer.

"No, all entirely legitimate," answered Yarr, looking away. "To be honest, I have gathered a good many of these bloods myself. Yes, I have been very busy over the years."

His customer walked slowly among the shelves, keeping his face hooded. He confidently moved a hand over the vials as he passed, clearly taking stock as he looked for something. As he observed the stranger, Yarr thought he recognized something familiar in his stature.

The customer stopped in the back of the store, where the vials thinned out and singular examples held primacy of display. "Do you possess a Fecund Exemplar?" he asked.

Yarin Yarr's winning smile softened. "Ah, that is indeed a very rare and particularly powerful talisman. What do you know of such an item?"

The customer turned toward Yarr, and while the hood still obscured most of his face, a wan smile graced his thin lips and his jaw was set like stone. "I am a collector."

"Oh, a collector, you say. Yes, I am not entirely surprised. I must admit, when you entered my store, I suspected as much simply by the way you held yourself, the way your gaze scanned past the common items to the more interesting vials. Now that I look at you more closely, I must ask: do we know each other? You do have a passing familiarity."

The customer shook his head and turned away.

"No? Very well," replied Yarr doubtfully, before returning to his banter. "But come this way, good sir! You have asked after perhaps the most intriguing blood I possess, that of a princess conceived at dawn on a summer solstice. I do not have much, but no one does. To be honest, I am unaware of anyone else stocking such an exotic solution at this time. It will not be cheap, even if I choose to sell it. Indeed, it is not really for sale."

"I can pay whatever you ask," offered the customer.

"No, it is not a question of money, my friend," replied Yarr. "One does not create a collection such as that which lines these walls without possessing talent, passion, and a touch of obsession. Certainly, the more common bloods—say, that of the ungulates and the servant classes—I part with easily. But the more special bloods, those I have obtained via a personal connection, often through their extraction . . . those I tend to keep for myself. Perhaps I would consider selling them to my friends, those whom I have come to trust and deem worthy.

"The blood about which you have inquired is an extraction of this caliber. If any vial here holds possession over me, it is that one. Why, you ask? As I have alluded, I drew this blood myself. I pricked the princess's veins with my needle and drew away the last moments of her life. Yet it is more than that. I knew it was dishonorable, but I couldn't help myself. I did it anyway, instead of perhaps saving her life.

"Of course, I cannot inform you of who the donor is. I mustn't! I'm sure you understand I am honor-bound to keep the utmost confidentiality where humans are concerned. Let me just say, she was a person of the finest grace. I had the pleasure of spending a season with her family at one of the royal estates some time ago. It was down in the southern lands of Shalalatah, so you are unlikely to know of whom I speak."

Yarin Yarr fell silent, his expression pensive. "It has been a long time. Let me tell you about this vial."

The sun shone down through swaying palms the first time I saw her. It was across the courtyard of the *Pallaczo Autreyr*. I sat in the corner amongst the men of the court drinking tea, imbibing thick smoke, discussing business, and arguing politics. She entered with her family. Now, of course I knew of her and her beauty—everyone did. Yet it was not until I witnessed her splendor with my own eyes that I believed the wild tales I had been told. None matched the reality of her exquisite grace. I recall staring into her eyes and being held with a piercing gaze.

Yet I get ahead of myself. At that time, I had traveled down to Shalalatah to escape the Captured. They were in the middle of yet another purge, and merchants of the mystic arts were high on their list of targets. The warm beaches and welcoming cities of the southern land called to me, and I set up a shop in Tarriq. I knew only a little of the people and their culture, yet quickly found my feet among the traders and courtiers on the *Pallaczo* grounds, most notably in the Cerise Corner where the merchants of the city gathered.

I discovered there were two small blood merchants in Tarriq, so I shut them down and ran them out of town. The first suddenly fell into trouble getting any new stock. The other? Rumors of blood infections can be surprisingly effective in killing a man's trade. These, followed by separate accusations of murder, quickly caused them both to flee. I know all my trade's weak points. It was simple, really.

Not long after that, I possessed my own shop. I settled in,

and business grew. I had developed some local contacts and was becoming a fixture at court. As is usually the case in any new location, the culture appeared quaint and without import, particularly since I kept myself distant and uninvolved. Yet I was sure to adopt their fashions, to keep a close-trimmed beard and wear loose cotton clothing, to learn their signs and make their symbols. And slowly, inexorably, the court drew me into its quicksand grip.

"Yarin Yarr," bellowed a large, imposing man as I entered the *Pallaczo* courtyard one morning and walked toward the bustling Cerise Corner. "Come, sit." He motioned with his thick arms at the empty chair beside him.

I acknowledged his greeting and took the seat. "How are we?" I inquired. Herk was a local supplier of arms and shields, a burly man not to be dismissed, neither by stature nor by reputation.

"My new friend, Yarin Yarr," he repeated, grasping my shoulder. "How is business here in Tarriq?"

"Good, good," I said lightly. "My clientele is growing."

"Excellent." He waved to a passing servant and ordered me a dark lime tea. I knew at once that I was about to be made an offer.

"That business when you first arrived," he said, squeezing my shoulder pointedly, then sitting back in his chair. "I understand it."

"I had to establish myself. I intend to stay."

"Certainly. That is good to hear. Otherwise, it all would have been too much if you had had only temporary plans."

I narrowed my eyes at him.

"No one noticed when you first arrived," said Herk, "but we couldn't fail to see you knock Vantce and old Gheyst out of business. It was masterful, to be sure, quick and precise in its results. Yet it was also a bit . . . noisy."

I sipped my tea. "How so?"

"Vantce was a young bull. People had high expectations of him, of where he would go in this town. And old Gheyst... Well, he was everyone's uncle. No one likes to see their uncle treated with such disdain."

I raised my eyebrows and nodded. "Yes, I see," I replied respectfully. I saw Herk wasn't intending to threaten but to inform. "I acted only out of a desire to do business," I stated. "There was no personal interest in the matter."

"How could there have been?" replied Herk. "It was clear you were a foreigner, unaware." He leaned in closely now, his breath laced with lime and alcohol. "There were some who wanted to step in, to remove you and restore the prior order. But I could see you were a man of skill and ambition."

I looked into his searching eyes and found a question.

"It took no small effort to keep the wolves at bay," he said.

I understood. Bowing my head, I thanked him, quietly and with genuine gratitude in my voice. I had acted on my own, but perhaps he had made it easier. "How might I repay this gift?"

Herk leaned back, his bulky frame relaxing. He nodded his head to the servant to bring another round of dark lime teas. "Yarin, there remains a complication in your situation. It is Vantce. He has not yet left Tarriq, and the boy campaigns for retribution against you."

"I see."

"I cannot do much more. He is at his lowest already, and while you intrigue me, I will do no more on your behalf. It would be too permanent, you understand?"

"I do not wish for the boy's pain or life," I made clear.

"Good, good. Then do me this favor."

"Yes?"

"Take him into your store under your guidance. He is

young and had some skill with bloods, before your mastery of the trade belittled him."

This request surprised me. "It is not usually a good idea to have one's enemy under one's roof."

"Indeed, this is true. Yet I think in this case, an accommodation can be made, no?"

I paused and thought about how to get out of his request. But I quickly saw a way to turn it to my own benefit. "It is always good to make new friends," I finally replied.

"Excellent!" bellowed Herk, and he leaned in once more. "Now I don't have to kill you," he growled with a wink.

We clinked our hot teas in steadfast agreement, and as the searing alcoholic beverage roared down my throat, I saw *her* enter across the courtyard.

First, let me say I had never before that moment felt an especially strong attraction to the fairer members of our species. Of course, I had had my dalliances, had found some very fine women to spend my time with, but none had caused me to pause—for time itself to pause—the way she did. I was unaware of myself, but Herk naturally was not.

"Let me provide you with today's final piece of advice," he said with a grin.

I turned and stared at him without seeing.

"It is dangerous to stare at the princess like that."

I quickly extricated myself from Herk's table and found myself walking toward the royal pavilion. Herk's advice bounced through my head, yet I was drawn to her. I had to see her properly, up close. At the entrance to the pavilion—a tall, carpeted tent—two armored guards crossed their swords before me and growled at me to halt. I did so with a start.

"Your business?" the more hostile guard demanded.

"I am Yarin Yarr," I announced with unfounded confidence. "I am newly arrived in Tarriq. I wish to offer my services to the king."

The guard looked at a pompous official behind the pavilion entrance, and upon receiving a curt nod, allowed me to pass.

The official rushed over and took me by the arm. "As you are undoubtedly unaware, being new in Tarriq, I advise you not to overstay your welcome here. The king and queen have no time for merchants, but your arrival has caused much gossip within the *Pallaczo*. You will have but a minute to present your . . ."

He led me into the inner chamber of the pavilion where the king and queen sat upon the royal dais with their children, and I have no idea what he said after that because suddenly she was seated before me.

Through an opening above the royal dais, the sun shone upon the canvas wall beside her and bathed her in radiant ruby-red. A soft breeze played through the chamber and ruffled her long, brown hair. Her delicate mouth curled in an expression of bored amusement, yet her bright-purple eyes stared at me intently.

I dropped to my knees and groveled before the royal family.

"Get up!" hissed the official beside me. "Do nothing without permission."

I rose to my feet and found the king and queen glaring at me. I bowed my head, but the king's sharp gaze had clearly assessed me in an instant and seen everything there was to know about me, namely that I was a fraud. That would never do.

"My great and gracious king!" I exclaimed, and bowed more formally this time with a flourish. "It is without doubt the highest point of my humble life to be in your most august presence."

I looked up from my bow at the king and saw his eyes brighten with intrigue. "I, your faithful servant, hail from northern lands, having been drawn south by word of your prosperous and beautiful kingdom."

The pompous official coughed impolitely, and I ignored him.

"With modest hand, I offer my unending service to Your Majesty and your family and your family's family. I am Yarin Yarr, Master of Bloods and purveyor of all their varied solutions." I stood up tall and smiled as widely as my mouth would allow.

The official sighed in annoyance and again took my arm. "Very well, Your Majesty," he announced, and pulled me away.

"Tell me more," said the princess, her raspberry voice sweet yet commanding.

I looked at her, again entranced. I longed to hold her. I felt the whole chamber pause, uncertain what to do. Herk's words echoed through my mind.

The pompous official ignored the princess and continued dragging me away, but the king cleared his throat, and the official stiffened. His grip released my arm. I stood before the royal family of Shalalatah with permission to proceed.

I would not ruin this unexpected boon.

I again bowed to the king, then resumed my widest smile and turned to the princess. "With your blessing, Your Highness, I will be honored to proceed," I said.

"Please do," she stated.

"Indeed." I drew myself up into a posture of authority. "The great and ancient art of drawing and enhancing the bloods of the world requires a sure and steady hand, and proves the key to many distinct advantages."

With sleight of hand, I produced a small crystal vial of crimson liquid from my pocket and held it aloft so it glistened in the sunlight. "This small sample of an enhanced blood is one of my personal specialties. Many enchant and mix bloods, but none quite like this. First, it can provide a person with a burst of energy and good cheer."

As I spoke, I popped off the vial's stopper, and I finished with a brief swig of the thick, burgundy concoction. A quick jolt of life bolted through me, compelling me to dance a tiny jig right there on the spot. "Ah ha!" I exclaimed. "Such a surprise—always! But that's not all."

Now I turned toward the princess and, full of courage, asked if she would like to volunteer to help. She stared at me with such disdain it almost overpowered the effects of my elixir, yet I persisted. I turned to my old friend the pompous official and grabbed his arm.

"My good sir!" he protested, but I forged ahead, quickly screwing on an atomizing cap I had hidden in my pocket and spraying him in the face.

At once, the anger drained away from his harsh features. He smiled at me and winked. "Hello," he said warmly.

I smiled back. "Now," I said with similar warmth, "that's much better, isn't it?" I patted him on the back.

"Absolutely. How may I help, my friend?" he asked in an earnest tone.

"You already have," I assured him. "Please, relax and enjoy yourself."

He nodded at me and wandered out of the room, singing a childhood tune.

I turned to the royals and once more drew myself up to my full height. "As you can see," I announced, "one small vial has myriad applications. I will now demonstrate but one more of many."

I held the vial up above my head, drawing my other hand down toward the ground and pausing for dramatic effect, then threw it down at my feet as hard as I could. With a sharp crack it exploded, and a thick cloud of red smoke shot up around me. Well-practiced in this finale, I leaped out through the doorway.

From the room behind me, I heard a gasp when a few moments later the cloud dispersed as quickly as it had appeared. As I left the royal pavilion, I slipped some coins into the guard's pocket. He grunted in appreciation, and I knew I'd be back soon.

Herk had left the Cerise Corner, but a young man sat in his place. It was Vantce. I had only seen the boy from a distance up until that point, but his shock of strawberry hair gave him away —that, and his dagger-sharp glare at me.

I walked up to the table and stared back at him. His eyes tightened, challenging me, and then he broke and turned away, mumbling something under his breath.

"Come with me," I ordered, and walked away.

I wasn't sure he would follow me, but as I left the *Pallazco* I started expounding my expectations of our situation. It was only after two blocks that I sternly stated, "I hope you can accept these terms," and turned back to face him.

His small knife hit my stomach like a thunderbolt, but I was prepared. The blade bent and slid sideways off the light silver-sheen armor I always wore beneath my cotton shirt in those days.

I twisted sharply, grasping his ear and scrunching it hard, forcing him to the ground at my feet. "Do not underestimate me, boy! This is the second time I have bested you. You won't survive a third time!"

I held his ear and waited. He squirmed as I pulled on it, willing it to detach, until finally he relented. "Yes," he muttered.

"What?"

"Yes, *mahti*."

"Very good." I released his ear, bent down, and helped him up. "Vantce," I said with some pretense of friendship, "from this moment, I mean you no harm if you work with me in our trade. Believe me, this can be beneficial to us both."

The young man rubbed his ear and stared at the ground, and then he slowly nodded.

"Very well. Come along."

After that day, he appeared before my shop every morning and worked as instructed without complaint until he was dismissed after sundown. I was firm yet fair, testing him and teaching him and correcting his poor techniques with blood. If I am honest, I will admit that his skill did show much promise. I sometimes wonder where he wound up.

At the same time, I used him to ensconce myself more firmly in the *Pallazco* and the princess's presence. I was drawn to her, compelled to see her and witness her beauty . . . but there was another motive underneath it all. Yes, you have already guessed. Of course, I wanted some of her blood. You already know that I was successful, but not how.

Months passed, and I was a common fixture around the beautiful seaside city of Tarriq. A lot of my work came from Herk, and through him, much more from the various dens around the city. Word-of-mouth also spread throughout the domestic households, and I gained a lot of business from regular concoctions based on common bloods such as eader and giant. I was at the *Pallaczo* courtyard daily, and was even in regular contact with the royal family.

I had the opportunity to see my princess most days, if only from a distance. On a lucky day, we might share the same room and maybe even a kind word, but it was always very stiff and formal. To be honest, I would not have had it any other way, not while the eyes of the court were always upon her, their radiant star.

She was, however, a valued customer who took great advantage of a number of my special blends. Yet I didn't trust myself, and I always sent Vantce to the *Pallaczo* with delivery of her orders. I heard she often spoke highly of me, and sometimes I received invitations for a meeting in her court. I wanted to attend. I wanted to stand in her presence and bathe in her glow. I wanted to hold her, to possess her—her and her blood. I believed I would find a way to obtain both of these things, yet was uncertain how to do so. I only knew that time was required, as well as patience and luck. We began exchanging correspondence in sealed envelopes, tucked in among the orders from the palace, and while I was always honest and open with my words, I was also aware these letters could be used against me.

One day as I stood in my store arranging vials into orders of potency, a royal guard appeared in the doorway. I stopped and inquired as to his needs, but he said nothing. He glared at me a few moments, then beckoned me to follow.

Outside, the sun had set and evening was descending over the world. The dusty streets between the white, terraced houses were turning light-blue. Children shouted in the distance as their games were interrupted by mothers calling them home. The world was at peace.

The guard led me to the *Pallaczo*, but not via a path I knew. We wound back along the outer walls and finally arrived at a creek that ran beneath them. He took me by the shoulder and indicated I should proceed along the creek.

"No," I said, but he gripped my shoulder more firmly and indicated the path once more.

A small ledge alongside the creek led me inside a tunnel. When I emerged on the other side, I heard a giggle. I turned around, suddenly angry at being made a fool, but it was her.

"Your Highness!" I said, dropping to my knees and bowing.

"Hush," she said gently, "and do stand up. There is no need for formality here."

I got to my feet and looked around to see who might witness this scene. We stood in a lush, green garden, carefully manicured to evoke wildness yet with every plant neatly positioned and trimmed. "I . . ."

"Do not be alarmed, Sir Yarr." She looked into my eyes like a tigress gazing at her prey. "There are none here but us."

"Yes . . ."

"May I call you Yarin?"

I stared at her, spellbound. With dream logic, she had asked to use my first name. "You can . . . call me . . . Yes."

"That's an odd name, 'Yes.'" She winked.

My knees trembled.

She pursed her lips and took my hand. "We don't have much time," she said, and looked around before leaning close. She smelled of coconut and vanilla, like a warm summer day. "Yarin, I've stolen this time to talk to you privately. There are things I've wanted to tell you that I couldn't write in our correspondence, and I have always felt your letters were also cautious. It was wise to be so."

In one of those moments that occur only once or twice in one's lifetime, everything cleared from my mind except the present moment. I took her delicate hand in mine and looked deeply into her eyes. "Since the moment I first beheld your beauty, I have been nothing but your servant."

She let me hold her hand and looked away, blushing as I spoke. "Do not think I did not notice. I recall your magnificent performance for my father every day . . . as well as the way you couldn't take your eyes off of me."

"Surely this is true of all in your presence?"

"Perhaps, but not like that. It was your soul I saw, not lust for money or power or congress."

"No, my dear, it was simply *you*."

We kissed, to my eternal surprise. My blood burned in my veins. My heart leaped in my chest. I drew back with a start.

"Surely this cannot be."

"It cannot. Nowhere but here. But here . . . maybe."

Noise rose up from within the *Pallaczo* grounds: the bell for supper and the murmur of voices.

"You must go now," she said. "But before you do, I have a gift for my favorite."

She drew a small blade from her bodice and held up the ring finger of her left hand. Then, with a wicked little smile, she nicked the tip. A small, burgundy sphere of perfect blood appeared. "Take it."

Ever ready in advance, I took a tiny vial from my pocket and captured the blood. Then I left her and returned to the regular world via the creek tunnel under the walls.

Our correspondence grew more charged after that meeting. Each letter became less guarded, emboldened by the knowledge that she wanted my words as much as I wanted to write them. The amount of blood she had given me was too small for anything useful apart from two things: providing proof of the majesty of her specimen, and keeping it in a crystal around my neck.

I didn't dare expect to see her like that again, but I held out hope I would. At court, she remained necessarily distant and aloof, apart from one time when we crossed paths amid a crowd and for the briefest moment our hands brushed. The gentlest hint of a squeeze was all I needed to know she saw me as I saw her. Still, I wanted her, and I wanted her blood. Having a good amount would allow me to create a solution more powerful than any made before.

. . .

It was my last day in Tarriq when my wish was finally granted. Vantce had delivered a selection of bloods to the palace as per usual, and when he returned, she was with him. I could not believe it. There in my lowly shop, she stood: the princess, cowled in a dark robe, hidden, beautiful. It was clear something was wrong.

"Yarin, you must help her," urged Vantce. His eyes were very worried, yet something hid behind them.

"Of course," I said, and took her into the back of the shop. I removed her robe and examined her. A light sweat covered her skin. There were black marks across her back and swollen glands under her left shoulder, and her left arm was limp. "What has happened?" I asked.

"I cannot say, Master Yarr," she murmured, "but Vantce told me you could help."

"I will try my best, Your Highness," I said, keenly aware of Vantce standing close by. "Please, I must inspect your throat. I mean no disrespect."

She opened her little mouth. I slowly raised my hand to hold her jaw and looked over her ruby tongue at the back of her throat. It was angry and inflamed, and as I had suspected a *jhestal* was lodged there, a small beetle I knew well. This insect was used for only one thing, which was not commonly known: to enhance the blood of a live source. It inevitably killed its host unless it was removed in time.

As for how it got there, I was at a loss until I looked at Vantce. The boy stared back at me with a malicious glare I had not seen upon his face since the day we had first met in the Cerise Corner. The day he had attempted to murder me.

I opened my mouth, but he spoke over me. "The princess is ill, Yarr. I am at a loss, but she asked specifically for you."

The princess's knees buckled beneath her, and I caught her and laid her upon a bench. I looked for Vantce, but he was gone.

"Yarin, help me," the princess whispered. She reached for my face, her gossamer fingers stroking my cheek. Her eyes were dilated. The *jhestal* was doing its job. As it pumped its ichor into her arteries, as she withdrew from this world into the nether, her royal blood thickened and fermented, enhancing its special properties. I had to get the *jhestal* out—

Yet as I reached for the long, thin calipers that could remove the beetle, my hand brushed against the syringe I kept beside this bench. Her blood was at its absolute peak at that very moment. I . . .

She coughed, deeply drawing her ragged breath and clawing at the bench. Reaching this late phase of the process meant almost certain death, but there remained a chance of recovery.

I caressed her head, held her face, stunned she was before me once more but horrified it was like this, at a loss for what to do.

Shouts erupted out front of the shop, loud and angry. A crowd bustled in the street. Vantce burst in through the store entrance waving a bunch of letters over his head. He scrambled toward the back, followed closely by furious guards and locals.

"He's in here!" he shouted. "He's killing her! Stop him! Tear him to shreds!"

There she lay, dead, alone. A small, red dot in the crease of her elbow was the only sign of my greatest sin.

"I let her die," admitted Yarin Yarr. "I'm sure I could have saved her, even if it meant letting that riotous mob hang me shortly afterward. Yet in exchange, I have this vial." From inside his cotton shirt, he pulled an ornate vial carved with the symbol of the rising sun: the Fecund Exemplar. "Her blood. The perfect hemoglobin."

The hooded customer stared in silence for a moment, then reached out to take the vial.

Yarin Yarr snatched it away. "You cannot have it, good sir. It is a blood of the rarest variety, and the power it contains cannot be expressed in words. It is not for sale."

"I wasn't planning on paying you for it."

Yarin looked at the customer, suddenly alert. "What did you say your name was?"

On this day, unlike the one many years before, Yarin was not wearing his light silversheen armor when the knife plunged into his stomach. He stumbled backward in shock against the overflowing shelves, grabbing the knife by its hilt, rueful that he had ever let his guard down. The vial hung openly around his neck.

The customer laughed and lowered his hood to reveal strawberry hair.

"Vantce!" exclaimed Yarin. "You found me!"

He was older, grizzled, but he still held that malicious glare, now accompanied by a nasty grin. "Indeed I did, you old fool," he gloated as he strode toward his blood-soaked mentor. "It took some time. You're a tricky one to pin down. Always moving, always alert. But you've finally lost your edge." He reached once more for the vial.

Yarin slapped his hand and moved away, his body pressed up against the shelves, vials rattling as he passed. He hadn't been entirely unprepared for such a moment, and he produced a small crystal vial of crimson liquid from his pocket and emptied its contents into his mouth. His eyes widened, and with renewed strength, he pulled the knife from his stomach and threw it directly at Vantce, who ducked and scrambled backward.

Yarin swore in agony, the deep gash in his stomach crippling despite the potion's effect. He sank to the ground, took the Fecund Exemplar from around his neck, and removed its stopper. Through gritted teeth, he poured some onto the gaping wound in his belly and swallowed the remainder. The enchanted solution entered his bloodstream through the wound, and he slumped sideways as he passed out.

One final time, the princess stood with him beside the whispering creek where they had met. Smiling, she raised her open hand in blessing. "I love you."

Vantce hid behind a cupboard, alert, awaiting attack, but nothing moved in the store. No sound was made. He ventured out and stood over the bloody body of Yarin Yarr, Master of Bloods. He snorted and bent down, scooping up the vial for which he'd made the long journey north.

"Too easy," he muttered, and spat on Yarin's body. "That's for Gheyst, you old bastard."

The ground at his feet quaked when he found the vial empty. He swore as the bloodied body tensed and rose slowly into the air. A shard of fear cut him inside as Yarin Yarr's eyes flickered open, shot through with strings of golden flame. Vantce fell back in terror as the air around the Master of Blood thickened and caught fire.

"Nothing to it," Yarr screamed, his voice demonic. He held his charred left hand palm-up before him; above it spun a drop of his princess's blood. He raised his flaming right hand at his enemy, and as Vantce's body started to combust, Yarin knew he was never to be human again.

About the Author

M. J. J. Moriarty is an uncharted author from Western
Sydney with a collection of fermenting
flash fiction, short stories, poems and novellas.
Formally educated yet entirely unprofessional,
you'll likely never hear of him again- he's allergic
to social media. "It's an honour," he muttered upon
learning his work was selected for this collection,
then went back to hiding in the sprawl from Roko's
Basilisk. His upcoming projects include an SF novel
concerning the future Emperor of Earth, and a
flash fiction about taking chances

The King's Burden

CHRIS MASTERTON

A soft breeze carried a gust of fresh air in through the reading room windows with the scent of blooming roses and freshly cut grass. The birdsongs of spring and the clear blue sky swept my imagination away from my lessons. Instead of listening to Master Delowitt, I was exploring the palace gardens, riding my horse through the woodlands beyond, and meeting with important dignitaries from far-off lands.

"Prince Edmund," Master Delowitt said sternly, snapping me back to reality. "Your Highness, I must insist you pay attention."

My tutor gestured toward the portraits on the wall. The largest depicted my grandfather, King Lecter III, ruler of Eltharnia. Underneath were my parents, then in a third, smaller row, my brothers, my sister, and me on the end.

"I know how the order of succession works," I said irritably. "Once my grandfather dies, my father will be king and Tranton will become archprince."

"Yes, and when Prince Tranton finally ascends to the throne, you will no longer be a prince, son of the reigning monarch. Instead, you will be bestowed the title of duke, along with lands and people to rule over in the king's name. Which means you must listen during your lessons!"

"A duke," I muttered. "Fancy title for a royal lackey."

"A great honor, Your Highness. One not to be balked at."

I sighed and looked out the window once again. I knew why Delowitt was lecturing me on this topic. "I heard that my grandfather's influence is diminishing. They say that he is on the brink of death. That my father will have a tough job to pull all of the duchies back into line."

Master Delowitt leaned across the escritoire and placed his hand on my shoulder. "You should never put too much weight in gossip. The king isn't dead."

"Yet." I sat back in my chair and crossed my arms. "It's fine, you can say it. Everyone has to die someday."

"But as you said, he isn't dead *yet*. Besides, your father will make a great king."

I rolled my eyes. "My brother won't."

"I'm sure Prince Trant—"

"Every time he or Albert sees me riding Spooky, they startle her so that she rears and I have to hang on for dear life. They say that's how she got her name: because she's so flighty. My brothers are always doing mean things to me. One time, they poured sand in my breakfast, and another time they put slugs in my pillowcase, and—"

"They're your brothers," Delowitt said, patting the air. "That's just what boys do when they're young."

"Tranton's twenty!"

"True enough, but he still has a long way to go before he becomes king. By then, he will likely have children of his own."

"Not if he fell out of a window and died."

Delowitt's eyes went so wide I thought his eyeballs might pop out. "Your Highness, you should never speak such words about your own family. If anything were to happen to your brother, I'm sure you'd be grief-stricken."

"Hardly," I sneered. "I'd be one step closer to being king."

Delowitt frowned. "Perhaps, but the likelihood of the rest of your family succumbing to freak accidents as well is highly improbable. Don't forget, Albert and Aveline are still ahead of you."

I nodded thoughtfully and cracked a sly smile. "So they are."

The next day, I went down to the stables early to prepare Spooky for the annual boar hunt. My father insisted on perpetuating the centuries-old family tradition, forcing my brothers and me to ride through the woodlands with the nobility in pursuit of some poor beast.

Spooky fidgeted about in her stall as I adjusted the stirrups, so I stroked her midnight-black coat and whispered in her ear until she settled. Fitting saddles and preparing the horses was usually the job of stablehands, but I enjoyed spending time with my horse. She had been a present from my parents when I turned sixteen, a Friesian mare from one of the best breeders in the kingdom.

"Someone finally found a use for you, eh, Ed-*mund*?" Tranton mocked from the entrance of the stables. Albert, ever at his side, laughed at the perceived slight.

I hated the way my brothers said my name like it was some sort of clever insult. "Go away, Trant. At least I know how to saddle a horse."

Tranton shook his head. "Whatever would I need to know that for? I can ride and hunt better than you, twerp."

Albert hoisted his hunting rifle, pointing it right at me. "I see a wild piggy, Trant. Should I make it squeal?"

"I wouldn't waste the bullet," Tranton scoffed. "Besides, I don't imagine he'd taste very good."

Spooky snorted and lunged against the gate in protest.

Albert sneered at me. "Better get your horse under control, *twerp*. That thing will be the death of you if you're not careful."

I glared at my brothers while they went to find their own mounts, already saddled by the servants, and rode out. Alone again, I put my foot into the stirrup and launched myself onto Spooky's back. Once settled, I pulled the lever on my rifle to open the breech and loaded a bullet into the chamber. It closed with a sharp click, and I slung the weapon over my shoulder before riding out into the yard.

The sun was still low, the morning dew just lifted. Everyone gathered in the cobblestone courtyard before my father led us out at a canter. I chose to stay at the back of the group, mostly to avoid my brothers, but also because I wasn't particularly interested in shooting a boar.

As the hunting party dispersed into the woods, the chatter and thumping fell away until it seemed almost peaceful. Soon, the chirping of birds overhead and the rustling of leaves prevented me from seeing or hearing anyone else. Spooky walked at an even pace, allowing me to take in the serenity.

After crossing a shallow stream, I spotted a horse without a rider, its lead wrapped around a thin tree. The chestnut stallion wore a royal-blue saddle blanket with my family crest embroidered on it. I guessed one of my brothers had stopped to take a break or relieve himself. I continued alongside a dense stretch of forest, and moments later heard something stirring in the thicket. Spooky shied away, and I tugged on the reins to bring her around.

"Trant? Bert? Come on, this isn't funny."

I couldn't hear their usual telltale snickering. My heart raced at the possibility that this could be something else. Something wild. I hadn't expected to come across an animal by accident. Even though I wasn't ready, I knew I would never live it down if I gave up the opportunity to take a shot, especially if my brothers ever found out.

I reached for the rifle, cocked it, and took aim. Trying to steady my breathing, I focused on the rustling in the thick shrubbery. A pile of leaves shifted as something leaped out of the bushes yelling and screaming. Spooky reared, knocking me off her back.

My head rang like a bell in my helmet as it struck the ground. It took a moment for the world to stop spinning, and when my eyes refocused I found Albert laughing hysterically, slapping his knees and pointing at me. He stood over me, still covered in leaves.

"The look on your face! I told you that horse is no good. Lucky you didn't break your neck, twerp."

My anger welled up. I wanted to scream at him and call him names, tell him how much I hated him. Then I realized I was still gripping my rifle, and a moment of resolute clarity engulfed me.

I sat up, took aim, and pulled the trigger.

With a sudden crack and a puff of smoke, a red stain grew across my brother's shirt. He looked up at me in astonishment. It was a good shot, right through the heart. Albert dropped to his knees, mouth still agape, then collapsed face-first onto the ground like someone play-acting a death scene.

I heard people approaching; the pattering of hooves grew louder, moving as briskly as possible through the dense bush. The riders no doubt hoped to get a glimpse of the first trophy.

"This way!" someone nearby exclaimed. "I see horses."

I sat, dazed, in the long grass where I'd landed. "Help! Over here!" I yelled, still clutching the rifle. "Albert's been injured."

More calls rang out as the message was relayed to everyone within earshot.

"Dear gods," one of the noblemen muttered, rushing to the body. A moment later, the man shouted, "He's dead! Prince Albert is dead!"

It still didn't feel quite real. At some point, a man I didn't recognize helped me up. My father knelt over the body, a stoic expression on his face. Tranton stood behind him, glaring at me in disgust.

My father stood and looked me in the eyes. "Edmund, what happened here?"

"He was rustling around in the bushes," I said, trying to appear innocent. "I thought it was a boar and drew my rifle, but then he jumped out at us. Spooky reared, and I went flying. My rifle accidentally discharged when I hit the ground."

The strange thing was, Father simply gave me a grave nod and walked away. No one seemed angry. They all just accepted that it had been a tragic mishap caused by another one of Albert's stupid pranks. On the ride back to the palace, I couldn't help but feel a great sense of relief.

I didn't see either of my parents again until the day of the funeral. A week had passed before Mother finally embraced me.

"My dear little boy," she said in a gentle voice. Her blood-shot eyes stared into mine. "I know this hasn't been easy for you. Just remember, it wasn't your fault." She had tried to cover her grief with makeup, but this close to her, I could see it was a mask. It made me wonder how much more of this she could endure. Father watched us with a stern expression, silently waiting until the royal coaches pulled up in the main courtyard.

Tranton joined my parents in the main coach while I rode

in the smaller one with my sister, Aveline. She sat across from me, her ponderous gaze fixed on the empty seat once occupied by Albert.

"It's all your fault, you know," Aveline said.

"No, it's not," I replied, perhaps a little too promptly. "You weren't even there."

"Doesn't matter," she huffed. "Of all the directions a stray bullet could have gone, you expect me to believe yours just happened to find its way into the middle of Albert's chest?"

"That's what happened," I said defensively.

My sister narrowed her eyes. I could almost hear her skeptical thoughts, but she said nothing more for the remainder of the trip.

The coaches pulled to a stop in front of the cathedral, where we were ushered up the front steps past the flocks of people who had turned out for the public service. My family and I were seated on the pew behind the bishop, with the exception of the sick king, who was noticeably absent.

The bishop appealed to the necessary gods before the full congregation, then gave each of us personal blessings for protection and good fortune. All the while, Albert lay at rest in his coffin like a monumental accusation. I imagined him entering the realm of the Great Beyond and calling the Gatekeeper a twerp. It almost made me laugh out loud.

After the service, we set off again, traveling deep into the countryside. The royal cemetery was an hour-long journey by coach. My sister remained silent for the majority of the trip, right up until the carriage jolted violently and both of us were thrown out of our seats.

Aveline screamed until the vehicle screeched to a stop. She looked at me wide-eyed and said, "Is it me, or do bad things happen whenever you're around?"

The carriage door flew open. "I'm so terribly sorry, Princess

Aveline," the coachman said, looking mortified. "Are either of you hurt?"

I shook my head and tried to peer out the door but could see only a valley of trees glowing orange in the setting sun. "What happened?"

"Some of the paths have eroded. We hit a pothole large enough to dislodge a wheel. I beg your forgiveness. I didn't see it until it was too late."

"It's fine," I said, glancing at Aveline, who was still fixing her disheveled hair. "We're fine."

"We'll be underway again in a moment," the coachman promised.

"Try to get us there without killing anybody," Aveline snapped, and the coachman retreated with a stiff bow.

It was dark by the time we finally arrived at the royal cemetery. The coaches stopped before the large iron gates, which creaked as the guards swung them open. Father led the way up the path, past giant headstones carved into fierce eagles, lions, and gargoyles designed to ward off evil spirits.

The crypt loomed over us, an ancient, creepy mausoleum that had been constructed generations ago. But this wasn't some dingy stone vault; it was a mansion in its own right, a building that put most people's homes to shame. Inside, the spacious rooms and halls were decorated with ornate draperies and portraits of my ancestors. Each chamber was the final resting place of some relative I'd never met. Their pristine, polished black coffins sat idly in rooms no one ever visited. One day, even I would end up here.

The royal guards hauled Albert's coffin onto a pedestal, and the bishop spoke a few words. Then everyone drank and told stories. Some cried, while others sat in quiet melancholy. I surveyed the room and carefully considered the three people who still stood between me and the throne. Father was stoic and strong, never one to let his feelings show. Tranton had lost his partner in crime, and this was the first time I'd seen him so vulnerable. Aveline, gentle and innocent, wept in Mother's embrace.

I decided to get some fresh air and wandered back down to where the coaches were parked at the front gate. The coachmen and royal guard had sheltered from the chill of the night in the gatehouse, where I could see them engrossed in a card game.

As I inspected the main coach—the one that would take my parents and Tranton back home—it occurred to me that I couldn't simply murder my entire family. On the other hand, tragic accidents happened all the time.

Every coach had a toolbox under the driver's seat, so I grabbed a wrench and proceeded to loosen as many bolts as I could without raising suspicion. Not so many that someone might notice, but enough that a hard bump in the path might jolt something loose. Once I was satisfied with the modifications, I slipped back into the wake with little more than a curious look from Aveline.

The ride back was agonizing. My stomach churned with butterflies and my mind raced in anticipation. Meanwhile, Aveline slept through the entire trip. If she suspected I harbored ill intentions, it wasn't enough to keep her guard up.

When we arrived at the palace, there was no sign of the main coach, so I found a dark room overlooking the courtyard and waited. It didn't take long until a lone rider galloped up the path, practically fell off his mount, and then ran inside.

I ventured out into the hallway, where sounds of alarm rose from the staff quarters. Although the words were muffled through the walls, I heard panic in the servants' voices and knew my plan had succeeded. My exhilaration mixed with dread as I realized there was no way to undo my actions. I had accomplished the unthinkable.

Somehow, I managed to sleep a few hours, then rose early and went to the stables before first light. Luckily, I knew how to get there without attracting any attention. As quietly as possible, I saddled Spooky and took off down the path.

Dawn broke by the time I found what I was looking for: two grooves in the gravel where the carriage had broken free of the horses and tumbled over the edge of a steep embankment. I stood at the top of the cliff, looked down into the morning mist, and saw the broken wreckage of the royal carriage. The place where my mother, father, and brother had met their untimely demise.

I thought about Mother. Her warm smile, her delicate floral perfume, her gentle hugs. Tears stung my eyes. It hadn't been necessary for her to die, but sacrificing her meant I was rid of my father and brother in one fell swoop.

When I returned, the stablehands removed their hats and stood sullenly as I rubbed Spooky down. In the palace, servants were huddled together, sobbing and consoling one another.

"Your Highness," the housekeeper said, rushing toward me. "We've been looking everywhere for you."

"I went for an early ride. What's going on?"

The old bird had dark bags under her eyes and used a handkerchief to wipe away her tears. She had never looked as weary as she did at that moment.

"I'm sorry, Your Highness, but . . . your parents," she said, fighting back more tears. "Your parents were in an accident last night. Their carriage came loose from the horses, lost control, and . . . well . . . They didn't make it."

"They're dead?" I tried to imagine how a normal person would act in my situation, but my mind snagged on an important detail. "What about my brother?"

The housekeeper placed one reassuring hand on my shoulder as she wept into her handkerchief with the other. "Prince Tranton was badly injured. The best healers in the kingdom are caring for him now."

I let the news sink in. At least my dismay was genuine. One accidental death wasn't all that suspicious. Two accidents were an unfortunate tragedy. But now I had to see this through by killing Tranton *and* Aveline, or it would all have been in vain. Each death made the circumstances more complicated, however. When I discovered that Master Delowitt had packed up his worldly possessions and arranged passage for himself on the first ship out of Eltharnia, I decided it would be best to lay low for a while.

After another round of funerals, Aveline and I went to stay at Rosewood Estate, my family's summer home by the ocean. It was far from the bustle of palace life, and the reduced staff made it feel as though we were almost completely alone. In the weeks that followed, I occupied myself with lessons and exploring the nearby town of Mills Port.

Aveline kept to herself, avoiding not only me but all other human contact. I often heard the maids whispering that she hadn't left her room in days. Then one evening, I went to dinner and found her seated at the dining table.

I tried for a pleasant smile. "Sister, I didn't expect to see you this evening."

"Why not?" she asked. "I have as much right to be here as you do. Besides, I'm expecting company."

"Very well then," I said, sitting down at the table and pouring myself a glass of scented water.

Aveline glared at me. "Something's different about you.

Ever since Albert's death, you've been . . . I don't know, more wooden."

"What does that mean? You never paid me any mind before. Why the sudden interest in my temperament?"

"Because you shot your own brother—"

I nearly choked on my drink. "That was an accident!"

"—and you don't seem the least bit sorry about it. Not to mention what happened to our parents!"

"Would you prefer it if I barricaded myself in my room all day crying about it like you?"

"That's not what I meant. I just want some indication that any of this bothers you."

I took a deep breath. "You think I had something to do with their deaths?"

She nodded. "I need you to look me in the eye and tell me you didn't. Promise me you aren't plotting to take the throne."

"That is ridiculous," I said firmly.

"Is it?" Aveline pushed her chair out and leaned on the table. "I saw you leave Albert's wake and come back with grease on your hands."

My heart started racing, and I stood abruptly. "I've lost my appetite. Good evening, sister."

As I walked away, I was acutely aware of her suspicious gaze burning a hole in the back of my head.

Once I was out of sight, I rushed to my room, heart still thundering in my chest, and retrieved the hunting knife I kept in my riding bag. The blade glimmered in the light as I unsheathed it and ran my thumb over the sharp edge. It was short enough that it didn't stick out beneath my jacket after I tucked it into my belt.

On my way back to the dining room, I went over the plan in my head, running through possible scenarios. Usually, the servants made themselves scarce once they had served the food.

Dinner was often the only time we had any privacy, so I knew no one would bother us. I tried not to think about Aveline as my sister; rather, she was just another obstacle in my way.

The dining room doors were closed, so I glanced around before flinging them open. Aveline started, placing her hand on her chest with a gasp.

"Edmund, what are you doing?" Her eyes opened wide, realization growing into panic as I crossed the room. "Please, just stop!"

She pushed away from the table awkwardly, almost tripping, and tried to retreat. I advanced until her back was against the wall. Tears rolled down her cheeks, and her breathing came short and fast. I tried not to think about her despair. This had to be done. Better to get it over with quickly.

I plunged the knife in.

Aveline moaned, her elegant, pink dress turning red as blood soaked through the fabric. I guided her gently to the floor, the fear and panic in her face soon replaced by empty calm.

A whimper came from the doorway. I looked up in alarm. A young lady around Aveline's age stood in the entrance, her hand over her mouth. She wore a long, lavender dress that looked expensive, so I knew she was not one of the maids. Then I remembered that Aveline had been expecting company, and my heart sank. In my haste, I'd completely overlooked that critical detail. I found myself reaching for my knife and judging the distance between myself and the door.

The young lady didn't run, didn't scream, just stared at me in shock. What was she waiting for?

"Your Highness," she said in an angelic tone, "you've made a terrible mess. Please allow me to help you clean it up."

"What?" I blinked rapidly and tried to focus. "You walk in on . . . *this* . . . and your reaction is to help me '*clean it up?*'"

"Would you prefer if I screamed?"

"No," I said, a little too forcefully.

The edge of her mouth curled in a slight grin. "Do you know the punishment for murdering members of the royal family?"

"Oh, please," I said, rolling my eyes. "And what do you get out of this? Blackmail? Leverage?"

"Power," she said flatly. "You're one more death away from becoming the archprince, and everyone knows the king isn't likely to see autumn."

"What is your point?"

"Make me your queen, and we can rule together."

I looked down at the blood pooling on the floor around me. The young lady didn't wait for my assent before acting. She closed and locked the door behind her, grabbed a cloth from the table, and handed it to me. It would take more than a napkin to clean my sister's blood off my hands.

"What's your name?"

"Lady Sienna, Your Highness," she said with a practiced curtsy and a sly smile. "Now, we should make haste."

Moving my sister's body was easy with the two of us, although cleaning up the blood took more effort. Then out the window and into the darkness we went. I fetched Aveline's horse from the stables without being noticed, and we used it to carry her body into the woods. Then I snuck back into the estate alone and ransacked my sister's room. When the maids went to wake her in the morning, they would find her personal possessions missing. It would appear as though—after weeks of melancholy—she had fled with her horse in the night.

After sunrise, to avert any doubt, Sienna rode back in tears with a tale of Aveline leaving in a fit of despair and Sienna herself pursuing the princess until her horse could gallop no farther.

. . .

From that night on, Sienna and I spent a considerable amount of time in each other's company. Although we were rarely alone, it often felt like we were the only two people in the world. The secret we shared, the smiles we exchanged, the knowledge that together we could seize the throne—it seemed as though we were a perfect team.

Then one day a letter arrived, closed with the royal seal. I broke the wax and read the precisely inked words on the gold-lined parchment.

"It is with the greatest regret that I must inform you that our grandfather, King Lecter III, has taken his final breath. A new star shines brightly over us in the night sky, where he now resides for the rest of time . . ."

For some reason, this news affected me more than anything I had done to my siblings and parents. That evening, Sienna snuck into my room and sat with me, her arms draped across my shoulders in silent solidarity. I looked into her knowing eyes and could almost read her thoughts. Only one more thing needed to be done, and then the kingdom would be ours.

The next day, we departed by carriage for the palace. I looked out the window, watching the rolling green countryside, and tensed a little each time the carriage hit a bump in the road.

Sienna sat on the opposite bench, studying me with a curious smile. "What's on your mind?"

"There isn't much time left," I said, feeling strange about speaking my thoughts out loud. "It will be hard enough getting time alone with my brother now, but once he's crowned king, it will be all but impossible."

"Not everything must be done by your own hand," she said, producing a small, clear vial from her bodice.

I narrowed my eyes. "Poison?"

Her smile turned into a devious grin. "You won't need to be anywhere near him. I can take care of everything."

"No," I insisted, "I want to be there when it happens. I want to see the look on his face when he realizes it was me."

Sienna's grin faded, but she never broke eye contact. "As you wish, Your Highness."

We both lurched as the carriage stopped and the door opened to reveal the splendor of the palace grounds. The coachman greeted us with a bow, and I stepped out first to guide Sienna down by her gloved hand. She marveled at the giant white pillars that stretched up to the pointed golden rooftops, each level of the palace lined with windows and balconies.

"You've never been to the palace before?"

She shook her head. "Not since I was a little girl. I barely remember it."

A page boy approached and bowed curtly. "Your Highness . . . your ladyship. The archprince requests your presence immediately."

"Not even king yet, and he's already treating us as his subjects," I muttered. Then, to the page, I said, "Tell my brother we'll see him once we've settled in."

He didn't move. "I'm sorry, Your Highness, but he asked me to escort you directly to his council room."

"His council room?" I glanced at Sienna.

"We wouldn't want to keep the archprince waiting, Your Highness," she said with a polite smile.

The page, probably not much younger than I was, let out a sigh of relief when I gave a short nod. He led us through the palace corridors in complete silence until we arrived at a room in the west wing that I didn't recall visiting before. The page knocked, listened, and then opened the door to usher us through.

Inside, Tranton sat behind an enormous oak table, dwarfed only by the size of the room. "You look well, brother," he remarked—probably the nicest thing he had ever said to me. "Lady Sienna, I presume? It's a pleasure to meet you."

Sienna curtsied deeply. "It's an honor, Your Highness."

Tranton gestured to the two seats on the other side of the table. "Please, sit."

I put a hand up to stop Sienna. "What's so urgent that you practically dragged us off the coach, *brother*?"

Tranton clenched his jaw, then took a deep breath. "Sit down," he said firmly.

I shrugged at Sienna and waited for her to sit first before occupying the second chair.

"I asked you here for two reasons," Tranton continued. "The first is to find out what happened to our dear sister."

"I've already written to you with a full account of the night she left," I said. "She spent most of her time secluded in her room. Then one night, she decided to take a horse and ride away. Nobody's seen her since."

"Just like that? She simply vanished without a trace, not even so much as a goodbye?"

"Your Highness," Sienna said, "I was with her the night she—"

"I didn't ask you," Tranton snapped. "Which brings me to my next point." He waggled his finger at us. "Whatever this is, whatever's going on between you, it's over."

"I beg your pardon?" I said.

"Begging my pardon is exactly what you should do. Your little summer romance is all anyone can talk about. We've had four deaths in the family, the princess is missing, and I am soon to be crowned king, yet *all* the focus is on Prince Edmund and some girl he found in Mills Port."

"So you're jealous, is that it? I can't pursue a lady's interest because you're worried I'll steal the people's adulation?"

"You know perfectly well it's not like that. Once I'm king, I'm going to make you Duke of Stenhalt."

"Stenhalt?" I repeated in dismay. "But that's one of the most influential duchies in the entire kingdom! Why aren't you giving it to Uncle Branton or Uncle Elmeir?"

Someone knocked on the door, and we all turned to watch a servant carry in a tray of tea and cakes. He poured three steaming cups and left without a word.

"Believe me, I have a plan for our uncles. But in order to keep Stenhalt in line, I need you to marry Lord Belmont's daughter." Tranton picked up the cup nearest to him and took a drink, grimaced, and placed it back on the table. "Don't look at me like that. Under normal circumstances, I'd be happy for you to marry anyone you liked. But after suffering through so much tragedy, we simply can't afford to take a casual stance with our vassals."

He stood up, reached for a walking stick leaning against the table, and hobbled over to the window. It must have been hard for him to let me see him like this. He leaned against the windowsill and stared out at the blue sky. "It's not just you, you know. I too will have to make a strategic marriage in order to secure our continued rule over this kingdom. Perhaps our children will garner better fortunes than we did."

I looked at Sienna and made sure she followed my gaze toward the cup. Instantly understanding, she slipped the vial from her dress and tapped several drops into Tranton's tea. It took but a second, then she was back in her seat.

"My heart bleeds for you, brother," I said to keep the conversation going.

Tranton turned to glare at me. "I'm sure it does." He limped back to the table and took another sip of his tea. "I know you don't like this situation any more than I do, but this is our duty."

I drank from my own cup and embraced the little flutter of excitement in my stomach.

After a lingering silence, Sienna said, "If I may ask, Your Highness, are you feeling quite well?"

Tranton looked puzzled, then thoughtful. Before he could answer, his lips began to tremble, and he loosened the collar of his shirt. His breathing became strained, and he grabbed at the table in an attempt to steady himself. "What . . . have . . . you . . . done?" he gasped, then fell off his chair and began convulsing.

"Get help!" I shouted. "Quickly, my brother has been poisoned!"

As Sienna scampered to the door calling for help, I knelt down next to my brother and said softly, "You're a real prick, you know that?" I paused to savor Tranton's wide-eyed expression of fear and betrayal. "You have always been absolutely horrible to me, so this is for all the times you made fun of me, pushed me around, and made me feel worthless. Now *I'm* going to be king."

His body went slack; his eyes gazed aimlessly at the ceiling. Everything after that was a blur. People rushed in, and someone checked his pulse. Sienna put her arm around me, tears streaming down her pale cheeks. A compelling performance. For good measure, I ordered the royal guard to round up and interrogate all of the staff, bitterly demanding that someone be brought to justice for this heinous crime.

As the nights began to grow cold, the kingdom reeled from the death of yet another beloved prince. The vial of poison turned up in a servant's room, and justice was swift. I had finally succeeded. Only my young age stood in my way. Yet there was still one thing that kept me from sleeping soundly. One more loose end to sever.

I rolled out of bed in the dead of night, donned my robe, and crept over to the door of my bedchamber. Everything was still but for the crackling fire in the hearth. Out in the hallway, the lush carpet muted my soft footfalls. I staggered down the wide halls like someone dazed from a dream and stopped at a familiar door.

I slid into Sienna's room with only the gentle click of her door latch to break the silence. She didn't stir.

The faint glow of the dying fire lit the room just enough to see shadows dancing across the face of my betrothed. I sat on the side of her bed and listened to her slow, even breathing. She looked peaceful. Beautiful, even. I ran my hand tenderly down the side of her face, feeling the warmth of her skin. I didn't want to do this, but it was necessary. Only then would my reign be truly assured.

I grabbed one of the plush pillows, placed it over her head, and pressed down hard, leaning into it with all my body weight. She thrashed about under the heavy blankets, but it was futile. I'd hoped that she wouldn't awaken, that she would go quietly in her sleep, blissfully unaware. Still, I didn't relent. Sienna had been complicit in two murders for no other reason than her desire to be queen, so what would happen when she got her wish? She was so much like me that I knew there wasn't enough room on the throne for the both of us. She would never be happy in my shadow, so she had to die.

After an eternity, she stopped fighting. Her body went slack. When I was sure she no longer breathed, I slowly removed the pillow and smoothed out her disheveled hair. She looked just as peaceful as she had when I entered.

I kissed her gently on the forehead and, with a long, deep breath, felt finally at ease.

A new day dawns and a soft breeze carries a gust of fresh air in through the reading room windows. With it comes the scent of blooming roses and freshly cut grass. The aroma is reminiscent of a simpler time. I wish I were outside exploring the palace gardens, riding Spooky through the woodlands beyond. Instead, I spend my days meeting with important dignitaries, forging alliances, and tending to matters of the court.

I look up at the wall that once displayed three generations of my family. Only one portrait hangs there now, all by itself. There I sit on my mighty throne, a magnificent crown of gold and rare gems atop my head. In my hand, I hold a goblet of red wine, angled so that some of the liquid spills out and trickles down over my fingers. On closer inspection, I notice that the dark shade of crimson resembles blood, and I wonder if I need to have the artist executed.

About the Author

Chris Masterton is a space nerd, tech enthusiast, and author with a 'healthy' addition to coffee. His interests involve reading and writing speculative fiction, mostly sci-fi. He enjoys exploring themes such as the future of humanity, artificial intelligence, technology's impact on society, and the meaning of life.

www.chrismasterton.com

The Mark of Oenna

RACHEL SPENCER

The night before her wedding to the Seneschal of Yverna, Miryn sat by her bedchamber window fingering the blade of a silver dagger while her twin sister wept inconsolably. Even though she understood Kisara's tears, irritation and resentment gnawed at her heart like rats feasting on a corpse.

Losing her temper at last, Miryn smacked the dagger down on the windowsill. "Oh, hush up, Kis! This isn't pleasant for either of us, but at least you'll have a life of your own after tomorrow."

"A life of my own?" Kisara choked out, swiping tears from her pale face. "What kind of life will that be when you're marrying the man I love?"

Miryn stiffened and turned to look out the window. In the distance, the snowy peak of Mt. Osetres jutted its ghostly silhouette against the night sky like the rotten fang of some mythical monster. "I can't help that you fell in love with Isim," she snapped. Then the ugliness of those words struck her, and her posture deflated. "I'm sorry, Kis. If I could change this, I would."

She heard the bed creak as her sister got up and padded across the room to her side. "I know, Mir, I know." Kisara hugged Miryn and pressed their damp cheeks together. "I wish we lived anywhere else—Avne or Dirondu, even the Raltish Wastes. Then we'd both have a chance at happiness."

"The Wastes are hardly a happy place, Kis. I wouldn't trade Yverna's mountains for endless acres of quicksand and swamp, no matter how much I want to avoid this wedding."

"I suppose not." Kisara pulled away from her. "But at least we'd be treated as equals there."

Miryn glanced down at the brand on her wrist that marked her as the firstborn, blessed of the goddess Oenna. All firstborn twins in Yverna were gifted in magic, but their counterparts were neither able to use magic nor true individuals in their own right—or so the priests of Oenna claimed. Secondborns were deemed living shadows of their older siblings, so while Miryn had been raised in luxury and taught by the finest tutors, Kisara had served as her handmaiden ever since she had been old enough to perform simple chores.

Few Yvernans seemed to question the goddess's wisdom, and Miryn knew many firstborn sons and daughters who treated their twins with contempt or, at best, the kind of indulgent affection one would reserve for a pet. Her heart had always rebelled against the custom, for she had seen time and again that her sister was more than an echo whose sole purpose lay in servitude. Kisara had her own preferences, her own thoughts, her own dreams and desires . . . as her love for Isim Evrihar proved all too well.

Miryn closed her eyes, trying to suppress the memories that flickered through her mind. A hot summer day not long ago, a garden drenched in white-gold sunlight that washed out the vibrant hues of the roses and dewflower blossoms. The sheen of a silk waistcoat had caught her eye, followed quickly by a glimpse of Kisara's auburn hair, then her sun-freckled arms twined around someone's neck.

Miryn's stomach lurched when she recognized the tapered line of Isim's jaw, the onyx ring on his right thumb that bore the seneschal's seal of office. She took a step back, in her haste kicking a small rock onto the flagstone path. The harsh, skittering sound drew the lovers' attention, and they jerked apart, faces flushed with guilt.

Miryn found that she could not look either of them in the eye, so she whirled around and fled, silk skirts tangling around her legs and sandals slapping against her heels as she ran. Kisara called out after her, but Miryn ran on, deaf to everything but the maddening buzz of her own thoughts.

At last, Kisara caught up and grabbed her hand, pulling her to a stop. "Wait, Mir, please. I—"

"There's nothing to say," Miryn interrupted, her gaze fixed on the wilting leaves of a hedge that needed pruning. "I don't love him, so why should I care whether or not you do?"

"Because you're the one who's going to marry him, not me." Sorrow laced Kisara's voice, but Miryn detected an undercurrent of suppressed anger as well.

"It's not my fault I was born first," she pointed out. "You know I'd trade places with you gladly if this damn mark weren't carved into my skin." She rubbed the crescent-shaped brand on her wrist.

"We could find a way to copy it."

"Oh, Kis, we've talked about this before. It wouldn't fool anyone, not without some way of transferring my magic to you as well."

Kisara frowned. "It's not impossible. The wizard does it every year when we send him tribute."

"Yes, and then we never see those people again! What do

you think happens when he strips their magic away, Kis? They *die*."

"You don't know that for certain. It's just as likely that he forces them to stay as his servants, or maybe . . ."

Miryn cradled her sister's face in her hands, gazing into the large, pearl-gray eyes that so resembled her own. "Ebras Unevahl is an evil man—no, not even that. He's a monster, living up on that goddess-forsaken peak with his stolen power and the frozen corpses of all the people he's slaughtered over the centuries. We will *not* share in that evil by using his methods, not even if it means that neither of us gets what we want."

"But this is the rest of our lives, Mir! We've never been allowed to want anything for ourselves—it's always been about following these idiotic customs, and it's made both of us utterly miserable. This marriage is even worse. Can you honestly bear spending your whole life with a man you don't love? I know I couldn't."

"It doesn't matter whether or not we can bear it." Miryn wrapped her arms around herself in a vain attempt at comfort. "The arrangements have already been made, and besides, you know what happens to secondborns who defy tradition."

Kisara's expression darkened, and Miryn knew she had hit a nerve. On their tenth birthday, their father had forced them to watch the maiming of a secondborn who had attempted to impersonate his twin as a warning to them both—Kisara for daring to insist upon her individuality and Miryn for indulging such heretical behavior in her sister. Kisara had become violently ill when she saw the boy's severed hand twitching in a pool of blood, and as she wiped the vomit from her sister's chin, Miryn had sworn she would never let Kis suffer like that.

But Kisara was nothing if not stubborn. Raising her chin, she pressed her lips together in a mutinous line. "What about

Jorn? He would take you back if you were free, I know he would."

"Stop it," Miryn whispered. The pain of walking away from Jorn was years old, but it still thrust a serrated blade between her ribs. "Please, Kis. You have to accept this. We both do."

Her twin had taken her hands and squeezed them tight enough to hurt. "No, we don't."

Now, the wedding was a mere twelve hours away and neither of them had come up with a viable way of stopping or altering it. Even Kisara, so fierce in her love for Isim, so determined to defy fate, had resigned herself to tears on this cool, late summer evening.

Miryn loosed a deep sigh and opened her eyes, wishing for the thousandth time that she had been born the second child, lacking in magic but free to make a life of her own once her older sibling had married. It would have been hard to be treated as a non-entity, of course, but she would have endured that happily to leave behind the stifling confines of duty and marry the man she loved. And what good was her magic when it could not erase the brand on her arm or open people's eyes to the needless cruelty of Oenna's cult?

Idly, she lifted a finger and called the magic forth, a cool trickle that rippled out from her core as though the clear waters of a mountain stream flowed through her. That smooth, liquid sensation was why the priests believed the power came from Oenna, she supposed, for the goddess was said to abide in the plentiful rivers and creeks that crisscrossed Yverna like the veins of some vast body.

In practice, magic had little to do with water—another reason Miryn doubted the religion. She concentrated on extending a tendril of magic outside her body, and it manifested as an iridescent shimmer that stretched from her fingertip to the dagger she had set on the windowsill earlier. It rose into the air and spun in a lazy circle above her fingertip, light glinting off the silver blade.

Kisara made an inarticulate sound and reached for the dagger, then stopped herself before touching it. "I don't blame you for wanting to keep this," she said softly after a moment, her gaze still fixed on the hovering dagger. "I wouldn't want to give it up either. It's so wondrous."

Startled, Miryn lost her grip on the magic, and it receded as suddenly as an ebbing tidal wave. The dagger fell to the windowsill with a harsh, metallic clatter that hurt her ears. "But I *would* give it up, Kis, you know that. I don't care about the magic, the prestige of being the seneschal's wife, any of it." She turned imploring eyes on her sister. "Please tell me you believe that. Please tell me you won't—won't resent me after tomorrow. I'm just as trapped as you are."

"So if there were a way to switch places, would you do it?"

"Of course!"

"Even if it meant doing something dangerous?"

"Yes," Miryn said, but the word came out strangely hesitant. Danger she could bear, but the look on Kisara's face, so fierce she seemed almost unrecognizable, made Miryn cold inside. "Have you found such a way?"

Her twin fidgeted with the skirt of her nightgown, slender fingers delving into the ivory linen folds as if seeking something solid to hold onto. "You won't like it," she confessed.

Miryn's eyes widened. "You don't mean . . . Kis, please tell me you're not talking about the wizard!"

Kisara crossed her arms and gave her sister a challenging stare. "Yes, the wizard. He's more powerful than anyone else in Yverna."

"But he's evil!"

"Then you won't go with me to petition him?"

"*Petition him?* Blessed river, he won't let you get a single word out before he kills you—or worse!"

Kisara didn't reply at first, simply gazing at her twin with pearl-gray eyes full of anguish and despair. "I'm sorry, Mir," she said at last.

Miryn took her sister's hand and drew her into a tight embrace. "So am I."

"But you're not sorry enough to do what's necessary," Kisara mumbled against her shoulder. Her voice sounded threadbare, sapped of all emotion. "I am."

Then, before Miryn could react, Kisara yanked out a small satchel from the pocket of her nightgown and dumped its contents over them both. Brown powder dusted Miryn's hair and face, filling her nostrils with a sharp, minty scent she recognized at once: starleaf weed, which their mother took each night to ensure sound sleep. Frantic, she tried to shove Kisara away, but the herb was potent in this quantity—her limbs already felt leaden.

"Kis, what—?" She coughed, hardly able to get the words out around her sluggish tongue.

"It's the only way," Kisara slurred, sagging against her. "Don't worry, Mir, we'll be happy now."

Still in each other's arms, the sisters slid to the floor as one, a tangled heap of linen and silk and sunset-colored hair. Miryn's heartbeat thundered in her ears as if trying to outrace the sedative she had inhaled. As her vision darkened, she saw a familiar figure enter from the adjoining room where Kisara slept. Her betrothed Isim, the man she had never loved, come to follow through on her sister's terrible plan.

Don't do this, she tried to say, but her muscles had gone too slack to form the words. *Please, Isim. Not the wizard. Anything but the wizard.*

She felt Isim's hands gently prying her and Kisara apart, and then she knew no more.

Ebras Unevahl.

The cruel name reverberated through Miryn's drug-fogged mind, rousing nightmares from the unnatural sleep that gripped her. She dreamed of a gaunt wolf of a man bending over her, the ice-white furs that cloaked his emaciated frame blending into the long, coarse mane of his snowy hair until she could no longer tell where the wolf ended and the man began.

Unevahl bared his teeth at her in a mocking grin full of serrated edges. Ice wizard, some called him, for the fortress he had built atop Mt. Osetres where the glacier never melted, and for his unfeeling heart that demanded a yearly sacrifice to fuel his search for the mystical Aziron diamond he desired above all else. And so it was that Miryn imagined Unevahl as a creature with colorless skin and cheekbones so sharp they pressed taut against his skin like knife-blades, his silver eyes glinting with the pale sunlight that glanced off the snowy slopes of his mountain home to pierce the unwary eye.

Leering, he seized her with frigid hands and slammed her onto an altar of ivory marble veined with frostbitten hues of cobalt and bruised plum. A scream caught in her throat as he raised an alabaster dagger above her heart, but she found her voice when his face blurred and shifted, transforming first into Isim's lean, handsome features and then into a eerie replica of her own. When her beloved twin plunged the dagger home, its blade was silver, its hilt contoured for Miryn's own hands.

The nightmare was real when she awoke. Even before her eyes fluttered open, she registered the hard, chilly slab of stone beneath her body and Kisara's voice murmuring nearby. Isim must have have given her something to counter the starleaf weed, for she sounded far more alert than Miryn felt.

"And you promise it won't kill her?" Kisara asked.

"Not if I leave a sliver of power within her," the man who must be Ebras Unevahl responded evenly. "The process is fatal only when a person's magic is removed in its entirety."

Miryn struggled against the waning effects of the herb to drag her eyelids open. Hazy shapes came into focus: a cavernous chamber, not white as she had expected but hewn from native rock in various dull shades of rust and earth. Deep alcoves in the walls contained large blocks of ice that glinted with a wet sheen, and in each one the frozen silhouette of a man or woman could be seen entombed in the merciless cold.

A tear trickled down her cheek. She recognized many of those frozen faces, not just the victims of Unevahl's annual tribute but others who had attempted to rescue their loved ones and died horribly for their courage. How could her sister believe such a monstrous lie when the evidence of the wizard's evil surrounded them?

"What do you want from us in return?" a third person spoke up, and Miryn's stomach clenched as she identified the voice. It couldn't be! Jorn would never be party to such a foolhardy scheme—never!

"From you and Seneschal Evrahim, nothing," Unevahl replied, a gloating undercurrent shading his tone. "From the twins, all I ask is a little blood. It would be best, of course, if both women agreed to these terms, but the younger can speak for both if her sister remains unwilling."

Multiple sets of footsteps approached, and Miryn found herself gazing up at Kisara, Jorn, and Isim, the three people she had trusted most and who had betrayed her in the name of her happiness as much as their own. But as dearly as she wanted to marry Jorn and gain her freedom, happiness could not be bought with such a vile bargain . . . could it?

"Can you sit up, Mir?" her twin asked, concern etching her graceful features.

Miryn made an incoherent noise in the back of her throat, and Kisara turned to Isim. "We should give her the chrysathia extract."

He nodded, then pulled out a small vial of clear liquid and tipped it against Miryn's lips. The syrupy substance slid into her mouth, its acrid flavor bringing fresh tears to her eyes. Moments after she swallowed it, her head began to clear and she could move again. Stiffly, she pushed herself upright, ignoring Jorn's attempt to help her.

"Leave me alone," she rasped, her tongue stumbling over the words. "Whatever foolish bargain you wish to make, you will have to do it without my consent."

A dark figure in her peripheral vision stepped forward, and she saw Ebras Unevahl clearly for the first time. Like his fortress, the wizard appeared quite different from the pale, unearthly creature of her imagination. His close-cropped hair was nearly as red as her own, his skin ruddy from the cold, and he had an average build that made him appear deceptively non-threatening. A closer look at Unevahl's narrow, hardened eyes and confident smirk, however, told Miryn all she needed to know about the nature of his power.

"The bargain is all but made," he told her. "I do not even require payment in full at this time. A few drops of blood now shall be sufficient, and even when I collect the remainder, I shall take no more than you can spare."

Miryn clenched her hands into fists. "And if I cannot spare any?"

The wizard's pale-blue eyes glittered like gemstones. "I think you shall find it otherwise."

Desperate, she turned to the others. "Do you truly intend to do this against my will?"

Isim's jaw clenched, but Kisara and Jorn looked away as if ashamed. Miryn tried again. "Kis, Jorn, please. You know this isn't right."

"Nothing about this is right, but we have a chance to fix that, at least for ourselves." Kisara took her hands and squeezed them tight, a half-crazed gleam in her eyes. "I can't let that chance slip by, Mir, not even if you hate me forever. But you won't be angry once it's done and you see how happy we all are. I *know* you won't."

Miryn tugged her hands free of Kisara's chilly grip and reached out to Jorn, who still stood with his head bowed, his tawny, shoulder-length hair hiding his face. "Jorn . . ."

He finally raised his head, and her heart stuttered when she saw the pain carved into his features. He looked almost as miserable as the day she had told him they could never see each other again. "I love you, Miryn," he said, and the strain in his voice sounded just like that terrible day, too. "I've always loved you, ever since the day you came into my shop to purchase that necklace for Kisara. No other firstborn would even think of buying such an expensive gift for their twin, but you . . . you have a heart more generous than Oenna herself, and I knew immediately that you were the only woman I could ever want. I've tried to be happy without you, but I can't. Please don't ask me to give you up a second time."

She closed her eyes against the sharp surge of grief that welled up beneath her breastbone. How could she choose between obtaining her heart's greatest desire and the evil that would accompany it?

Unevahl laid a heavy hand on her shoulder. "Whether you agree to this or not, it *will* happen. Why not give your consent and, by so doing, purchase greater happiness for yourself and your loved ones? Clearly, you desire a new life as much as they do."

Miryn drew a shaky breath. "My consent is that important?"

"It would lend the spell greater power, yes. The willingness of the subject is always preferred, although it is not a requirement."

"Then I suppose you have my consent." If resolve mattered so much to the wizard's dark magic, perhaps her wariness could blunt whatever evil might come of this bargain. After all, as he had said, she could not stop it, and it would be far worse if someone discovered their ruse because the spell turned out to be insufficient. "Take what blood you will, wizard."

The wicked edge of the smile that spread across his craggy face disturbed her, but it was too late to withdraw her permission. "Then lie back down, and your sister shall join you."

Biting her lip, Miryn stretched out on the stone slab, and Kisara clambered up onto the slick surface beside her. Unevahl directed Kisara to position herself with her head at Miryn's feet so that the twins were opposite to one another, then drew an alabaster dagger from his belt. Miryn started when she saw this, for it was the only item so far that had mirrored her nightmare.

Seeing her distress, Jorn stroked her hair back and offered her a reassuring smile. "It will be over soon," he murmured.

The soothing words could not stop the sickening roil of Miryn's stomach or the runaway pace of her heartbeat. She stretched out as far as she could and managed to brush her sister's hand. Kisara reached back, and they clung to each other by the barest tips of their fingers.

Unevahl made a pair of shallow cuts on Miryn's wrist above and below her brand, then did the same to Kisara even though her skin was still unmarked as yet. He collected the blood they shed into a ivory bowl, then used that blood to paint arcane symbols over each woman's heart.

When he began to chant, the river of magic that had flowed through Miryn's veins since birth drained away, not the gentle stream she knew so well but an icy, raging torrent tearing her asunder from within. She shrieked and writhed on the stone slab, and a moment later, Kisara's screams joined her own as all that power flooded into her body. Gradually, Miryn's brand faded while the skin on Kisara's wrist took on the crescent mark that signified Oenna's favor.

At last, it was done. Unevahl fell silent, and the agony faded. He picked up the ivory bowl, in which a small puddle of the twins' blood remained, his expression stoic. "The transfer is complete. Nothing remains to identify the true firstborn but the fragment of magic she must retain in order to survive. Go and reap the benefits of your sacrifice."

He turned his back on them and left the room without another word. Jorn and Isim helped the sisters up, and all four of them huddled together for several moments. Wearily, Miryn watched Kisara run her fingers over the indented skin on her wrist, eyes full of hope and wonder. Miryn felt hollow, not just siphoned of magic but of all vitality.

"We should go," she said. "If we miss the wedding tomorrow morning, all of this will be for naught."

Isim gave a brisk nod and wrapped an arm around her twin. "It will take several hours to reach the city, but if we push the horses, I am confident we will arrive in time."

He and Kisara began to walk toward the arched doorway on the far side of the room, but Jorn hung back. "Be glad, Miryn. I know this was unpleasant, but our life together will be worth it."

He touched her cheek, the pads of his fingers rough and cracked from shaping metal links into the elaborate jewelry he sold in the artisan's market. She had always loved that gentle, abrasive sensation against her skin, how it sent sweet shivers all the way to her core, but now it made her want to weep. Although they had purchased a lifetime of such delights, she dreaded the consequences. One day, Unevahl would return to collect the remainder of the blood she and Kisara owed, and she did not trust his claim that he would not take more than they could spare.

In the way of all things, time lessened Miryn's fear little by little. Kisara stepped seamlessly into her new role as firstborn, and although Miryn often sensed Unevahl's scrutiny upon her, she resolved to seize whatever happiness she could. And she *was* happy despite the lingering resentment that ached like a half-healed wound in her chest, for she loved her husband and sister dearly, and she could not deny the joy they had found in their new lives.

In truth, she might have forgotten the wizard entirely if not for the unsettling fact that she and Kisara seemed to mirror one another more and more with each passing year. When her twin wrote to say that she was expecting her first child, Miryn herself was already pregnant, and when the time came, they each gave birth to a son on the same day.

Seven years later, when she and Kisara found themselves once again pregnant at the same time, Miryn told herself it was mere happenstance. After all, nothing terrible had come of it the first time. Her son and nephew were healthy, their lives untainted by any threat that she could discern. Surely the wizard had forgotten about the bargain, for why else would he wait so long to demand his due?

One night near the end of her term, she lay awake in bed beside Jorn, the baby kicking ceaselessly inside her as though trying to pummel its way free of her body. Despite the stifling summer heat, stealthy tendrils of cold wound about her limbs. An unnatural torpor took hold of her, and her eyes slid shut.

When she opened them again, it was as though no time had passed since the night before her planned wedding to Isim Evrihar. She recognized the slick, frigid surface of the stone slab she lay upon and the rough-hewn walls with their corpse-filled alcoves surrounding her. She fumbled for Kisara's hand, and the two sisters held onto one another by strained and aching fingertips, just as they had before.

"Kis," she whispered, "can you get up?"

Cloth rustled as her twin tried to shift position. "No."

The baby kicked again, and Miryn gritted her teeth to hold back the pain. "Neither can I."

"What's happening? Why are we here?"

"Presumably, Ebras Unevahl intends to collect on our bargain."

"But why now?" Kisara sounded even more panicky than Miryn felt, her voice on the verge of cracking. "What if taking our blood hurts the babies?"

"Why would I harm your children?" Unevahl's question echoed throughout the cavernous room. Miryn craned her neck and caught a glimpse of his robed figure approaching the altar at an unhurried pace. "They *are* your blood, are they not?"

Miryn's heartbeat faltered, then picked up speed. Beside her, Kisara gasped as the wizard's meaning became clear.

"That was not our arrangement." Miryn tried to sound calm, but her words came out breathy and wavering.

"Ah, but it is what I bargained for," the wizard replied. He reached the altar and set down a familiar ivory bowl. "Since you did not specify what form your payment would take, I am free to choose the manner in which the debt must be satisfied."

"But you promised you wouldn't take more than we can

spare!"

"Nor shall I. Each of you already has a child. In time, you shall not miss the ones I claim for my own."

A guttural cry of rage tore out of Kisara, and the air around her shimmered as she tried to use her magic to lash out at Unevahl. Miryn held her breath, remembering how it had felt to wield such power, an endless river coursing through her body. But the iridescent bands fluctuated violently, then dissolved like rainbows dissipating into mist. Kisara whimpered in pain.

Unevahl gave them a ghastly grin. "The pact was sealed by blood—the blood in your veins, that is. It cannot be broken, not even by my own magic. I'm afraid you will have to resign yourselves to my terms."

Icy tears trickled into Miryn's hair, matting it against her temples. "What if . . . what if you drain my blood after the baby is born? All my blood, the last of my magic, everything I have to give—it's yours as long as our children are safe."

"And mine," Kisara panted. "You can have mine too, if you let the baby stay with Isim."

The wizard shook his head. "A noble offer, but one that would do me little good. For generations, I have availed myself of the magic of firstborn twins throughout Yverna, but it has never been enough. Now, through the linking spell I performed on you ten years ago, I have created a set of twins who shall be born to two different mothers, both the first to leave the womb that nurtured and carried them, both to receive Oenna's blessing." A dreamy smile crossed his face, and he raised his hands in the air, fingers opening and closing as if attempting to grasp the intangible power he hoped to acquire. "But do not fear: they shall come to no harm. Rather than stripping them of their magic when they come of age, I shall raise them as my servants."

Miryn bit her lip to hold back a painful sob. "But—"

"No." Unevahl lowered his hands, and the beatific expression on his face hardened. "I shall take the children of your blood, and the unprecedented strength of their dual powers shall be mine to command. Nothing less can breach the spells that protect the Aziron diamond, therefore your children are the only payment that can suffice."

Kisara moaned, but Miryn tried one last time. "What if they are not twins?" she asked desperately. "Or what if only one of them bears Oenna's mark?"

The wizard's lips twisted into a cruel grin. "You should pray that she favors them both, for if not, death shall be the only recompense possible: yours for reneging on our deal, and your children's for failing to fulfill their purpose."

Miryn flinched at the threat. As her twin's sobs reached an earsplitting crescendo, all of the resentment she had suppressed for the past decade boiled up within her. Once again, Kisara had forced her into a situation where she had no choice, only this time there would be no happiness for either of them.

Miryn squeezed her eyes shut against the miserable future she saw unfolding before their family: Jorn and Isim's horror when their wives returned to them no longer pregnant, the empty ache in all their hearts that no other child would ever fill completely, the harsh words and blame that would tear them apart, the rescue attempts that would end in another set of frozen corpses for Unevahl's grisly collection.

But consent mattered, she remembered, her hands straying to the swell of her abdomen as if to caress the baby she would never hold. Perhaps, if she were lucky, giving permission might buy her child an iota of the happiness they would never know otherwise.

She opened her eyes and met Unevahl's pitiless gaze. "So be it, wizard. Take what you will."

About the Author

Rachel Spencer has been writing fiction since she was old enough to hold a pen. She is part of the creative team behind <u>Twisty Tales from Tornado Trap</u>, a quirky kids' series about the adventures of a disaster-prone Texas town that is set to launch in late 2023.

http://www.twistytalesfromtornadotrap.com

Blood will have Blood

ILONA KRUEGER

Shelley took a last look at the house of her childhood. She sighed as she handed the keys to the real estate agent. This moment was even more difficult than the funeral. She drove back to her apartment, the twenty-minute drive seeming farther and lonelier than she remembered.

A couple of glasses of wine and some chocolate later, she flicked through some family photographs, adding a stream of tears and nostalgic smiles to the equation. The old record player that only ever got played on a Saturday afternoon or special occasion, outdated now but stored in the favorite memory corner of her mind. The old toaster with its flip-open sides which required on-the-spot vigilance. The Hills Hoist clothesline hung with freshly-washed linen swirling and dancing in the breeze, the end result of hours of laborious work. She could still remember her mother diligently overseeing its installation while her father did all the work digging the hole and mixing the concrete. Worrying, with sweat on his brow, that the impending rain would ruin his efforts.

Soon the Hills Hoist would be pulled down to make way

for a streamlined entertainment area. Her childhood home now belonged to others, people whose hearts and souls were not embedded in the walls, whose laughter did not brighten dark corners, whose secrets did not lurk under the floorboards. Soon these memories would be cast into the archaeology of the future.

Dandelions and clover had taken over the backyard, a childhood wonderland of weeds that had given countless hours of fun, and sometimes pain. The sting of a bee, bullets of bird muck on the head, and the prick of sticky paspalum being pulled off hairy legs. But the hiding spots for games, the trees for adventure, and the boggy puddles for splashing when it rained had outweighed any negative moments.

A thought straggled into her mind and niggled at her, a vague secret, a promise of some sort, but what was it? She wracked her brain but found no enlightenment.

A week later, in a dream, she remembered: the time capsule buried beneath the Hills Hoist! And then urgency pervaded. She had to revisit what, as a nine-year-old, had been held sacred in that time capsule.

"This is a building site!" one of the workers yelled as Shelley tried to squeeze through an opening in the temporary fence. "You must leave, otherwise the company will risk a huge fine,"

"I need to get something I left behind. Please, it's important. I won't be long—I know exactly where it is." She pushed past him, heading for the backyard armed with a small hand shovel and a plastic bag.

Scowling, the worker balked her way, but Shelley was unfazed as determination guided her steps over piles of sand, gravel, timber, and tools. To her surprise, the demise of the rotary clothesline had already occurred. It lay there in a sad heap. Digging around the gaping hole from which it had been extracted yielded no results. Could she have remembered wrongly? She dug furiously, unaware of the unamused looks of the nearby work crew.

"It must be here! It was in a sizable metal tin, and it was wrapped in plastic. It can't be gone!" Surely the fifty years that had passed wouldn't have disintegrated her prize into nothingness.

"You looking for this?" One of the men pointed to what looked like a small boulder covered in soil, insects, and slugs. He gave it a sharp tap with a shovel. The metallic clang told her that it was, indeed, what she was looking for. The relief she felt at retrieving her treasure outweighed any embarrassment or annoyance she had felt at their mockery.

"Oh my God, yes. That's it!"

"Must be something pretty valuable there. You a pirate or something?"

Shelley laughed in spite of herself. The sight of an almost sixty year-old groveling in desperation over a filthy-looking box with contents of no commercial value must seem pathetic.

"Valuable to me and no one else. It's a time capsule, and to tell the truth, I have no idea what's in it. I was only a little kid when we made this big important ceremony about what is, no doubt, no longer relevant." She took the box, brushing off a snail. As she did, she noticed her hand was bloody despite no injury.

Strange.

The others noticed it, too. "What did you do to yourself?" one of them asked. He held out a bottle of water and a clean wipe from the first aid kit. "Need a Bandaid?" The worker turned her hand over, inspecting it, but he too could find no injury.

"I'll be fine," she said with a dismissive laugh.

Her phone rang. It was her boss. "I need you to come in as

soon as possible. Short notice, but it can't be helped. Three of the others have called in sick."

So much for her plans. The box would have to wait. She stowed it behind the driver's seat and made a mad dash home to get changed into her uniform.

Work was usually a thirty-minute drive in light traffic, but within minutes traffic came to a standstill. That was all she needed. Probably a collision or breakdown. A quick but illegal U-turn set her on an alternative route. It would be a bit longer, but that was better than being stuck.

Dark clouds loomed overhead. Strange. The early news hadn't forecast rain. In the very moment the thought came to her, some drops dotted her windscreen. Fortunately, it was a short but heavy shower.

As the windscreen wipers dried off the excess droplets, she felt a knife-like sensation brush against the back of her neck, and instinctively she knew that if she were to move, it could be lethal. But of course, it was only her imagination. Nevertheless, she reached back and touched the painful area, recoiling in shock as she felt the stickiness . . .

Blood!

And yet she could feel no wound. Was she losing her mind? Once again, however, her hand was covered with it. Shelley had heard of strange phenomena such as bleeding statues and weeping paintings, but she had always looked toward a scientific explanation. She and other skeptics simply thought it was something orchestrated to dupe people.

Lost in thought, Shelley found herself in unfamiliar surroundings. She was nowhere near her work place. Had she taken a wrong turn? She always drove the same way to work, but this time, she was lost.

She switched on her GPS, and the voice announced, rather too joyfully, "You have arrived at your destination!'

She was outside a graveyard!

The GPS kept repeating the same words, stuck in what appeared to be an endless loop. She pressed the button to turn it off, but it kept repeating, "You have arrived at your destination!"

She switched off the ignition, relieved when the infuriating message finally stopped. She checked the maps app on her phone, then did a U-turn to head back in the right direction.

"You win this time," she thought she heard someone say.

Several hectic hours of work later—her head pounding from complaints, impossible orders, children running around screaming, chairs scraping too loudly, and cackling laughter— Shelley arrived home. There hadn't even been time for a bath-room break. She longed to flop down with a glass of wine and some television, but her own kitchen needed attention.

As she shuffled dirty dishes, a steak knife fell, narrowly missing her foot. Shelley picked it up carefully and put it on the counter. For the third time that day, she found blood on her hands—and yet, no wound. She would have to see a doctor if this persisted. Perhaps she was developing some kind of blood disorder. Maybe she was in the throes of hemophilia. Researching on her phone for a few minutes indicated the unlikelihood of that.

Shelley finished clearing the table, rolling her eyes when she saw her unfilled prescription for blood pressure tablets. She had already missed two days and had been warned against skip-ping them. A trip to the twenty-four hour pharmacy was in order. It was only a few streets away.

It began to rain again as she left the house. She turned her wipers on to no avail. The rain simply smeared across her line of vision, and within minutes, completely obliterated her view of the road. Shelley stopped the car, grabbed a few pages of an old newspaper, and investigated the situation. She rubbed hard until the glass was once again clear. From the peripheral light of the headlights, she could see that her hands were stained.

That's what the newspaper does, she observed, but a closer look sent shivers up her spine. Her hands were yet again blood-red. This was not hemophilia or a mere coincidence. This was an attack. But from what? And why?

Even worse, she was parked outside the graveyard again. Something was shepherding her there. *Like a lamb to the slaughter,* she thought.

Not usually a negative person, Shelley smothered the thought but knew instinctively that she had to get out of here. Something sinister was happening . . . unless it was her imagination. But the building site workers had witnessed it, too. It was not her imagination. It was real. Something she could not yet explain, possibly something dangerous. Sooner or later, she would find out. But did she want to?

She fled back to the relative safety of her car while the words pounded out, half-mocking, half-warning, "Second time lucky. Three strikes, and . . ."

Since she had no shift scheduled for the next day, Shelley looked forward to a day of puttering around. A few menial tasks had to be done, and then she would look at that box, which was still in the back of the car.

Relegating her misgivings to the backburner, she retrieved the box as soon as time allowed. She felt like a child anticipating the arrival of Santa Claus. Obviously, it would require a bit of cleaning up after all those years trapped underground. But, she reflected, treasure chests were nearly always worth the effort.

Lifting it out of the plastic bag, she almost dropped the whole thing. Lines and pockets of red slithered around the contents. She could only surmise it was blood, and yet nothing like that had been visible yesterday. Her excitement and anticipation were wearing off, and she considered simply bagging it all up for garbage.

Curiosity, however, would not allow her to do this, so she braced herself for what the contents might disclose. Perhaps some dark, evil force had intercepted it at some time in the intervening years, or someone was playing a horrendously unfunny joke on her. The construction workers? They wouldn't have known she would arrive to retrieve it. Then who?

Bracing herself for what she would discover in the box, she stood in freeze-frame for several minutes before she could gather the courage to continue. It was, after all, only harmless child's play. Something to do with blood kin, as had been the popular trend back then. Silly kid's stuff, just for fun, a faded thread of memory.

The longer she deliberated, the longer the suspense and fear would engulf her. She had to know. It was now or never. Using an old pair of scissors, she cut the covering carefully, avoiding contact with what she felt in her gut was blood. She put on some surgical gloves, but nausea swept over her nevertheless. This was irksome. She was surprised she hadn't spewed her breakfast yet. Was all this really worth it?

The covering now off, Shelley tried to pry open the latch. It seemed to have fused shut. A few sharp hits with her hand trowel didn't help. She gave the box a good shake, and sickeningly, some maggots made their entry into the daylight. What was inside this thing that promised such a stomach-turning revelation?

Armed with a pair of tiny jewelry pliers next, she tried to

wrench open the latch, straining her hands and arms until she felt she'd been in a wrestling match with a heavyweight champion.

Frustrated, she toyed with the idea of throwing the whole damn thing over a cliff, or at least into the trash. After all, there was nothing actually valuable in it that was worth salvaging. But determination didn't allow for that.

A search for her container of more substantial tools came up with nothing. Not in the trunk of the car. Not in the laundry. Not in the garage. Not under the bed. Surely not in the freezer or bathroom? Where were they? Then it dawned on her. She had loaned her tools to a friend who was now away on vacation, so there was no chance of getting them back quickly.

After a short drive to the hardware store, she was soon equipped with a pair of strong pliers, some Loctite glue remover, and a can of insect spray to kill those ghastly maggots. Her one-time role as a nursing assistant should have prepared her for such unpleasant sights.

When she was homeward bound once more, a bout of nausea overcame her, causing her to stop the car. And here she was again . . . at the graveyard. This was unbelievable. The graveyard was nowhere in the vicinity of either her home or the hardware store. She felt like she was being led there by an unknown force for a purpose she did not know.

A voice crashed into her awareness. "You cannot get away this time. Follow the blood trail, and you will receive understanding. Ignore this, and you will be next."

A warning! Next for what? Death?

Like an obedient servant, she followed the trail, which led to a grave. Heart pounding, she read the inscription and was surprised to see a familiar name: Kathy Palmer, a helpful childhood friend who had lived on the same street as Shelley.

Memories of the small group that had made a harmless childhood pact surfaced.

The blood trail took her to another grave. The words were similar to the other headstone: "Departed this world in an awful and untimely manner." And there it was: Mandy Bourke, the other girl in her group, whose laugh had been like a tinkling bell.

When the trail diverted farther into the graveyard, a feeling of trepidation overtook Shelley, initiating a spontaneous run for her car. But something dragged her back, guiding her feet, forcing her along a path she didn't want to take. As much as she fought against it, it was as if her body had been overtaken by some malevolent being, an entity that was not her.

It led her to an open grave with fresh soil in a large mound beside it, surrounded by flagging to prevent any mishaps. A labeled signpost was staked at the end. There was a date and a name: *her* name. And the same words: "Departed this world in an awful and untimely manner." Her spine chilled, her blood froze, and her heart felt like a huge ice block, cold and dead. Sheer terror ordered her to run. This time, the unseen force allowed her to leave the cemetery and drive home.

What did it all mean? She sensed it was connected to the time capsule. Nothing weird like this had ever happened before. Although she dreaded the contents of the time capsule, she desperately wanted to find out what mysteries lay inside.

What had happened to the other two girls? From the dates on the inscriptions, she surmised that their deaths had occurred soon after she had moved away to get married. That jogged her memory. There was a vague recollection of her parents mentioning a murder years ago, but nothing specific had been said. Her mother had signs of early-onset dementia, and her father had never paid attention to details such as the names of her acquaintances and friends. Shelley's own job, her new

BLOOD WILL HAVE BLOOD

circle of friends, and the immediacy of everyday married life had occupied her time fully. She had only returned to Brighton after her divorce because her parents needed her. A lot had happened since then.

Eventually, with a bit of force and Loctite, Shelley was able to get into the time capsule. Within, she found a few trinkets: a bead bracelet, a dancing ballerina from a music box, an overseas coin, and a trick plastic finger marked with fake blood. She shivered when she saw it. It was wet. The blood was real. How could this be, after it had been sealed up all these years?

There was also another small box completely sealed with tape. Shelley put it aside for last. She moved on to an envelope, yellowed with age but overall intact. She pulled out the written message within. The childish scrawl had been marked with red pen.

BLOOD OATH

We solemnly swear never to double-cross our blood kin.
We promise to keep secrets and not tell even our parents.
We promise to be friends forever.
Time will tell.
Signed:
Kathy Palmer, age 9
Mandy Bourke, age 9
Shelley Williams, age 9
Phillip Randall, age 10

At the end, each of them had pressed a bloody fingerprint next to their name.

They had all been in school together, living in the same neighborhood. Friends. All in the same grade, although Phillip was marginally older. The first two girls were dead, presumably by some horrific means. The vows meant nothing, just stuff that kids do, and yet two of them were already in the ground. Shelley wondered if it would be weird for her to try to track down Phillip.

She became aware of a presence in her house. An unexpected draft prickled the hair on the back of her neck. An uncanny feeling that she was being watched prompted her to look around and check each room of her small villa. Nothing untoward. A window was open, and a light breeze ruffled the curtains. She shut it. Nevertheless, she still had an uneasy feeling. And who wouldn't? Blood out of nowhere. A car that took her to the graveyard. Voices that threatened her.

She needed to eat. She needed coffee, maybe even a strong drink to help unwind. Some chill-out music, or a movie on Netflix. One thing was for sure, retrieving that time capsule had been a mistake.

She gathered up all the bits and pieces and stashed them in a plastic bag. Then she wrapped another bag around the whole lot to make sure the contents were well-contained. Tomorrow, she would dispose of it as far away as possible. But what if she were led to the graveyard again? No, she would walk, put it in a trash can behind an old warehouse, and be done with the whole deal.

Even after a meal and a glass of port, Shelley could not exile the disturbing concerns from her mind. There were no logical or scientific explanations for the events of the last couple of days. If only she hadn't been so sentimental about a rusty old tin. She flicked through all the television options and could find nothing that appealed to her in her preoccupied state, scrolled through her phone reading comments on stupid memes, and checked a couple of friends' timelines. Everyone was having fun, out for dinners and parties. Everyone except for her. Here she was, by herself night after night, as if she were socially inept.

On a whim, she Googled the names Kathy Palmer and Mandy Bourke to see if anything could shed light on what had happened to them. She found several newspaper reports, all of which ran along similar lines. Her speculations were confirmed. They had been found gruesomely stabbed to death in their early twenties. So very young. Phillip Randall had been the prime suspect, but he had never been charged. A jury had dismissed the case due to lack of evidence. Which meant he was out there. Free. Free to kill again. And she was the only one left of the three girls.

She shuddered as she recollected the open grave with her name on it. But what was the motive? What had brought him to murder? How could she have missed all this? Kathy and Mandy had been her friends. She reconciled her guilt by conceding that life directions and new horizons often cause people to lose contact. Nevertheless, she had failed them.

Enough speculation. She needed to realign her thoughts. Her eyes searched the room for ideas.

Shelley suddenly remembered her yearbooks. Of course! Eager to see whether they contained any clues, she settled herself at the kitchen table. The small, sealed package was still where she had left it.

She half-smiled. *It can't exactly walk away,* she thought wryly. Best to open it now and have it done with. The contents would be a surprise. Phillip had been furtive about it, saying, "Secrecy binds the magic." The girls had laughed. They'd called him Mr. Mysterious.

Upon opening, the package revealed a men's pocket watch, an old wind-up one. It was in perfect condition, with no corrosion on the casing, nor any condensation within the faceplate. And what's more, it was still ticking. After fifty years, how was that possible? These watches needed winding daily, unlike the modern battery-operated watches which kept going for a maximum of two years on average. A perpetual watch. Just like Time itself.

It was a beautiful piece. She wondered whose it had been initially. Perhaps Phillip's, given to him by his father or grandfather, a precious legacy. But why would he place this in a time capsule which might never be found? Did it show that Phillip trusted their friendship for all time? Perhaps he had stolen it, therefore it was something easily given away to make himself look cool. But since none of them had seen what the sealed package contained, that didn't make sense. The other explanation might be that he had hated whoever had given it to him, and he had seen it as a ritual of riddance.

Shelley turned the watch over to see if there was an inscription to suggest ownership. No names or initials could be seen, but there was a symbol, hardly discernible without a magnifying glass. She had one among her sewing tools. A close inspection revealed a bird, a phoenix whose body and head were represented by a dagger.

She shuddered. What did it mean? Phoenixes rose out of their own ashes, it was always said, and daggers were obviously connected with death. So what was supposedly magical about it? Of course, there was no denying that weird things had happened since she'd retrieved the time capsule. Nevertheless . . .

Too many thoughts. Too many possibilities. But the thought that Phillip Randall could have been responsible for the vicious deaths of her two friends lingered. Nothing could excuse such horrible deeds. Vague recollections of Phillip hovering around them years after their pact sprang into her mind.

She skimmed through the pages of the yearbooks. No real

clues there, except for the message Phillip had left in her final yearbook. "My aim is for fame, and in time it will be mine." Chillingly prophetic.

Shelley pulled her sweater closer to her body. A group photo captured her attention. Phillip was standing by himself to one side, but instead of facing the camera he was staring at her and the other two girls with a wolfish, hungry look in his eyes. It scared her. She had never noticed it before, but now that she was focusing on it, she could not unsee it. If only she could go back in time as an observer, she might be able to get some insight into what had made him into the dangerous person he seemed to have become.

She picked up the watch that was tireless in its purpose. Lightheadedness overcame her, and in moments she was aware of spiraling through space and time, as if in a dream. And then she was there, in the woods where they had all gone one evening, presumably to welcome the first full moon of the New Year, the Wolf Moon.

It was unusually warm for winter. A midnight picnic had been planned, and the girls had brought food. They were miles away from home. Phillip had driven them, wanting to impress them with his recently-acquired driver's license.

Phillip had brought wine, but it seemed very potent, and in retrospect, she wondered if it had been tampered with. His behavior had seemed oddly flirtatious, maybe as a result of the alcohol. At first, the girls had laughed and told him to stop being silly, but they quickly became uncomfortable when he initiated some unwelcome and sleazy advances. Intuition told them to bring their planned ceremony to an early conclusion before it deteriorated any further. Their long-term friendship with Phillip seemed to be evolving into something they did not want.

Phillip was not easily deterred by their resistance. "Chill, girls. Just have a good time. Life's too short to have rules. Come on, then, you're all sixteen, old enough to have a bit of fun." He guzzled another mouthful of wine straight from the bottle, spilling half of it down his shirt.

The girls huddled together in a knot to protect each other as he became more insistent.

"This should be an initiation into adulthood. For old times' sake. After all, we promised to be friends forever."

"This is not what friendship is about. We trusted you," Kathy piped up.

"If you don't, I'll spread the story that you've been sleeping around," he sneered.

"And who's going to believe you? We're not the ones who already have a bad reputation," Mandy blurted out.

"Nasty—!"

"We felt sorry for you when you lost your mother last year. We made allowances, but you're not the person you were when we were kids, so take us home. The night has been spoiled." Shelley summed it up. The other girls agreed.

"And if I don't?"

"It won't look good if we have to walk back, hitch a ride, or freeze to death," Mandy said in a low tone. Then she gave a sudden order: "So take us home! NOW!"

"You'll be sorry one day, you'd better believe it!"

And yet, day after day, he still tried to hang on to them possessively, growling at any other boys who might show an interest in one of them. He hovered and shadowed, never missing an opportunity to exert control. They warned him off many times, threatening to report him, and it eventually came to the attention of the principal, who directed Phillip to desist or face consequences.

After that, he had been less than congenial. "You're just a bunch of snitches and liars," he'd accused.

They hadn't reported him. Someone else had. He'd been observed . . .

Suddenly, Shelley felt herself spiraling back into her older body. As she found herself once again in her own lounge room, she wondered whether or not there was, incredibly, something true about the magic Phillip had alluded to. But then why get rid of it? Her head hurt. She tried to talk herself through this, but something unsettling disturbed her peace.

A low-toned voice filled the room. "I will get you. I knew you'd come back. I've been waiting. I've been waiting for so long . . ."

She looked around, wondering where it was coming from, but she found nothing. Was it in her mind?

The next day, she rid herself of the time capsule, and hopefully of its negative effects. She realized it would not change the fate of her two school friends. They had paid the price. Should she now escape, move away, to avoid any chance of crossing paths with Phillip again? Or should she voice her concerns to the police? Would they even listen?

She needed to do something to calm her escalating fear. She should get some groceries or maybe wander through the shops, perhaps even have lunch in a café. Her shift was not until later in the day, but there was no reason she couldn't indulge herself a little, put the horrible revelations behind her. Explanations for some things were not always forthcoming.

"You won't get away, so don't fool yourself. You are just as guilty." The same low-toned voice resonated throughout her car.

She switched on the radio and turned the volume up high to drown out the accusations. Maybe she needed to consult a psychologist. There had certainly been a lot of pressure on her these last couple of years. Her imagination was going crazy, but she refused to let it gain power over her.

Deep breaths. Distraction. Determination.

Groceries, a meal she didn't have to cook, a new outfit. Shelley was set for renewed positivity. She would get herself a job in the city, do a course or two, find new friends and new activities. Maybe even some love. She had spent so much time looking after everyone else's welfare that she'd forgotten her own.

She collected her mail: a few bills, some advertising brochures, a couple of requests for charitable donations, and an actual letter. That was rare these days. She filed what she needed and threw the rest into recycling. The letter would have to wait until after her shift. The better part of her wanted to call in sick, but she needed the money. Reluctantly, she dressed for work.

Many hours later, she returned home, too exhausted to even eat a proper meal. She flopped onto the sofa with a packet of chips, a can of Coke, and the unopened letter.

There was nothing on the envelope that could have prepared her for the contents. It seemed quite formal at first, referring to her by title and surname. Seconds later, however, her equilibrium failed.

Her mind fizzed. She was a balloon, all air rushing out. Frantic attempts to catch her breath failed. Cold sweat drenched her. Faintness threatened to engulf her.

In disbelief, she read the letter again and again through blurred vision, yet was unable to make any sense of it. It was from the cemetery office. It appeared that her request for the plot in D section was approved, and was ready now for imminent burial of . . .

No! She hadn't made any such application. She shook her head as her mind grappled with the name that followed. Not again! Her name in full! This had to be someone's idea of a joke. A sick joke.

"I am not dead!" she yelled out. "Do you hear me? I. AM. NOT. DEAD!"

"But you will be, and sooner than you think."

Where was this voice coming from?

Then she saw him as he emerged from the shadows.

Alarmed, she jumped up, looking around for escape, but he was blocking the only exit. She tried to calm the pounding in her chest. "What are you doing here?" she demanded, then said more shakily, "Get out of here. Leave me alone."

"You want to know what happened to our friends? They got what they deserved. Ungrateful wretches. But you made yourself scarce. Where were you?"

He advanced upon her with slow, deliberate steps, each one bearing down deliberately as if he were killing snails. He had always done that. He had always been cruel.

She saw the blade. It glinted menacingly in the light as Phillip held it up for her to see. He was going to kill her! Instinct told her to make a run for it, but with nowhere to go, all she could do was arm herself with a weapon. She grabbed the letter opener.

She tried to reason, to bargain, to sidestep. "I have your watch. It's beautiful, a real treasure. Don't you want it back?"

"Do I look that stupid? The watch will always be mine. It has done its job. I've found you. I came here to provide a cold, empty grave with a warm body." Evil glinted in his eyes. He was not to be deterred. The dagger was now firmly in his grip. "Enough of these games. Time for revenge."

Shelley dropped the watch, and in one unplanned motion stomped on it with the heel of her boot, grinding it onto the floor—an impulsive action that surprised even her. Maybe she did it to hurt him, maybe to show him that she would fight, or maybe to somehow harness her anger.

And to harness him. In moments, he had disintegrated into the shadows, his voice resounding with an ear-splitting "Noooo!" that would always remain in her memory.

Shelley didn't sleep at all that night. She surfed the internet randomly. A page popped up without prompting. *"Phillip Randall, double-murder suspect, dies in car crash on lonely highway."*

The date? Five years earlier. She tried to access the rest of the article, but it disappeared.

It didn't matter. She gathered up the fragments of the pocket watch and threw them in the trash. It was time to move on. There was nothing for her here.

The next day, Shelley packed her things.

About the Author

Ilona Krueger lives in the Nepean Valley, in Sydney, known for its stifling summer heat. She writes poetry and fiction, largely for herself, but variously published. Several novels are in process, contending with her other assorted interests of gardening, imagining, needlecrafts, dreaming, pen pals and creating. Her dollhouse is awaiting furbishing. Her toy room brings back childhood delight. Although German is her native language, she taught English, History and Languages for many years. Now it's time for coffee.

Magick Mirrors

STEVEN DUTCH

"**O**MNACRA-ZOH-ES-AH!**"

Ben sat at his father's feet, feeling nervous. Cold sweat dripped from his brow and rolled down his face as he quivered on the concrete floor of the basement. All was dark apart from several candles lit around him in a circle. Mirrors lined the walls on each side, reflecting the dim glow of the candles.

Anthony stood over Ben with his arms wide and his head tilted back, looking up. He remained in that pose for a long time, waiting for the ritual to begin.

With a crack of lightning, a small portal opened near the roof and a tornado stormed out, swirling around the father and son. Black and purple smoke spun through the growing maelstrom, and small sparks flowed out, zapping around the room to electrify the air. A radiant, golden figure emerged and floated down toward them.

Anthony brought his hands together with a sudden clap so loud it ricocheted through the room and caused Ben to jump. He observed the stout figure looming over him, suddenly unable to recognize his father. This crazed stranger draped in the long, baggy black robe wasn't the man he knew at all.

"This is it!" Anthony cried out in anticipation. He lifted a long, curved dagger to the sky and sliced it across his hand. Blood dribbled down his arm, and he let it drip onto his son's head.

Ben squinted, wiping the blood from his skin. It burned like a brand on his forehead. The humidity wrapped him tightly, pressing on his chest and forcing him to heave. He bolted to his feet and ran into the hallway.

"Wait!" Anthony called. "Where are you going? We haven't finished yet—"

"Whatever you're doing, I'm not finishing it!" Ben shouted over his shoulder.

The door slammed, leaving Anthony alone. The glowing figure continued to descend.

Where is the subject?

"I'm sorry." Anthony sighed. "He escaped, so we will have to try again later."

There is no later. I am here now.

"We can't finish the ritual without him—"

There is no time for this. We must finish before the seal of manifestation opens, but I don't have a body to possess!

The translucent, glowing orb drifted within eyeshot of Anthony, who looked perplexed and worried. "Ben was born as the moonchild, designed and consecrated to be your earthly incarnation. His is the best body for you to take. I'm too old, and my body won't accept you. Where will you go?"

The entity did not respond. It floated down through the floor, where a dog was giving birth in the dark, damp passage beneath the house. The entity glided into the puppy's body as it was born. Instantly, it raised its head, eyes glowing like fierce, golden embers.

. . .

Ben slammed the door to his room. He ran his hands through his hair and held his aching head. Did this pain have something to do with the ritual he had just experienced, or was it the plethora of thoughts rushing through his mind? Either way, his head was pounding, and he wanted it to stop. Tears trickled down his cheeks.

Ever since he could remember, Ben had been subjected to the strange rituals his father conducted. Since he had never met his mother, this was all he knew. From everything he had managed to piece together over the last several years, it seemed that he had been born as the result of a ritual conducted by his parents, but something had gone wrong and his mother had died during his birth. He ran through the theories in his head again, but he couldn't formulate any solution to his problems when there was so much missing information.

A light rap sounded at his door. Ben spun around, frantically rubbing the tears from his eyes so his father wouldn't see them.

No one entered the room. He walked to the door and cracked it just enough to peer out. There was no one there. Slamming it shut, he turned around in a huff. He jumped in fright at the sight of two glowing eyes peering at him from under the bed.

"What the hell?" Ben yelped.

Slowly, a small dog emerged. It was no more than a puppy, light-brown with darker patches around its stomach and tail.

You have nothing to fear. The words weren't spoken so much as formed in his mind.

Ben stammered, "Y-you talk?"

I'm not sure I'd call it talking. More like communicating.

The puppy licked its paws, looking up at a rather confused Ben. *I do many things.*

Ben stood silently for a moment, contemplating everything that had happened. "Why are you here?"

I am here to help you, for I am the great spirit Aiwass.

"Aiwass?" Ben said. He vaguely remembered reading about the spirit in one of Anthony's many occult writings. "What do you want with me?"

You are at a crossroads, and your decisions will impact the development of not just this world, but many worlds.

"Many worlds?" Ben wondered if this was some trick his friends were playing on him, although he didn't see how that was possible. "My decisions about what?"

You are special. You have the opportunity to end so many wrongs. It all depends on what you do with the knowledge that has been given to you.

"What would you know about that?"

I am here to guide you to the righteous path. I can help you illuminate yourself, regardless of what your father has done to you.

Illuminate myself? Ben scratched the back of his head, deep in thought. He had often wondered if such statements were mystical nonsense. "How do I know I can trust you?"

You don't. But what can I do to you that would be worse than that which you have already experienced? If you do not act on this now, it will be too late. You must trust me.

Ben nodded slowly, and the puppy came to sit at his side.

Sunshine flooded through the partially-drawn curtains, bathing Ben's face in the warm glow of morning. He stretched, letting out a groan as he rubbed sleep from his eyes.

The day is ripe with possibility.

Ben rolled over and looked at Awaiss. "Oh, you again. I was hoping that was all a dream."

I realize I am dreamy. Aiwass sat up, looking proud and his wagging tail. *But dream you did not. I am here to help you.*

"And how do you plan to do that exactly? You don't know anything about me."

You greatly underestimate me.

Ben wasn't sure how to respond. He rubbed his eyes again, trying to gather his thoughts. He couldn't continue like this. He rummaged through a pile of paper on his desk, trying to find the brochure he had brought home earlier.

"The only thing I can think of is to go here." Ben showed Aiwass a flyer for a church.

Aiwass shook his head. *Exorcizing demons?* The dog let out a snort. *Humans! You always believe something evil is happening. Do you honestly think your father summoned a demon into you? What evidence do you have for such?*

"I don't really know what he was doing, but I bet— Wait a minute. Why am I explaining myself to a dog?"

You know you don't actually need to speak out loud to me. You will look quite insane if other people hear you—talking to a dog.

"How do I speak to you, then?"

Just think it.

Like this?

There you go.

Wow, I didn't know I could do this!

Everyone can, but not everyone has someone with whom they can communicate.

I'm not sure I like this.

And why is that?

Ben shook his head as if clearing it of cobwebs. "It's very confusing."

Just then, Anthony called through the closed door, "Breakfast is ready!"

Ben swung his feet off the bed and stood. "Well, I'd better go down there, or he'll realize something is up."

After yesterday, he will definitely *think something is up.*

Ben threw on some clothes and went downstairs to the kitchen. Anthony was already seated, fork in hand. "Good morning, son!"

Ben remained silent as he sat down at the table, eyes on his plate. Aiwass bounded down the stairs, stopping at the bottom. He looked up at Anthony and Ben with a spark of joy in his eyes.

"I see you've made a new friend. What's his name?"

"Uh . . ." Ben scratched his head. He didn't know if he should confide in his father. "Fido."

Aiwass gave him a dirty look, which he ignored.

"That's a nice name," Anthony said as he passed syrup across the table. "I made your favorite: French toast cut into bite-size pieces."

"Dad, I'm not a kid anymore," Ben hissed. "I can cut up my own toast."

"I know. I just wanted to do something nice for you."

"Trying to make up for something?" Ben asked snidely as he picked up a knife and fork and started to eat.

"About that . . . I wanted to have a discussion." Anthony rubbed his nose and cleared his throat. "You know I only want what's best for you, right?"

"That's the thing." Ben stopped eating and looked at his father. "How on Earth was *that* best for me?"

"There are a few things I haven't told you," Anthony started, then froze up. Tears welled in his eyes, and he wiped them away. "Your mother and I had a plan for you. We started it a long time ago, and she died trying to complete it. I need to finish it, otherwise she died in vain."

Ben pushed his plate away and stood up. "Don't start with that crap. Tell me exactly what you were doing and why—and don't give me some bullshit about Mom, either."

Anthony went quiet. His mouth moved but nothing came out, like he was choking on his words.

"That's what I thought!" Ben shouted, then stormed out.

He rushed to his room and stuffed a few things into his backpack. Aiwass waited for him at his bedroom door. On the stairs, Ben rushed past his father, who was coming to talk to him. Aiwass followed in a playful trot. As Ben darted out the front door, he heard Anthony shouting after him, but he wasn't listening anymore. His father had never explained anything before, so why would he start now?

Ben sprinted down the road with Aiwass not far behind. They got halfway to the next street before Ben slowed down.

What now?

"We go here"—Ben pointed to the address on the church pamphlet—"and see if they know how to fix me."

There isn't anything wrong with you. Well, nothing that's not wrong with all humans.

"Thanks for your concern," Ben said sarcastically. "You know what I mean."

They walked along the street until Aiwass stopped at a fire hydrant. Lifting his back leg, he let a stream of urine flow.

"What are you doing?"

What does it look like? Marking my territory. Everyone needs to know who is king around here.

"And that's all I know," Ben told the priest. "I've been left in the dark all my life, and now I can't take it anymore. My dad did another weird ritual on me last night, but I ran out before he could finish."

"Hmm, sounds like black magick to me," the priest said softly, stroking his chin. "And what of this . . . Aiwass?"

"He's right here." Ben gestured to the dog beside him.

The priest glanced down, then shook his head and turned to the man behind him. "There's definitely something wrong if he believes he can communicate with a dog."

The other priest replied, "It's obviously a way to dissociate from whatever was done to him."

"No, he really talks! Say something, Aiwass."

Panting, Aiwass sat up and barked.

The priest turned back to him and said in a mocking tone, "Oh, look, Raul, a talking dog."

The two men laughed, but Aiwass closed his eyes and a strange kind of energy moved through Ben. He felt Aiwass's presence within his own body, and his face began to burn.

The priests gasped, their mouths open wide. "Look at his forehead!" Raul exclaimed. "Is that . . . ?"

"He's definitely possessed," the first priest finished.

Raul's voice broke as he said, "We need to exorcise him immediately. It looks like the boy's father tried to instill a demon into him."

The priests grabbed Ben by the wrists and dragged him into another room. Ben resisted, but couldn't break free of their grip. "Hey! What are you—?"

The priests slammed him onto a bench. "We need to get this devil out of you. Then you will be fine."

They tied his hands down, then walked away, leaving Ben struggling against his restraints. Aiwass walked around the room and found a chair on the other side. He gnawed it, trying to rip it to shreds.

"Would you stop that and get me out of here?" Ben said.

What would you have me do? Overpower them with my cute face?

"Cut the sarcasm," Ben said. "How can I escape?"

Don't worry, I have a plan.

"Oh great, you have a plan. Would you mind telling me—?"

Without warning, the priests stormed back in, swinging censers full of incense and chanting, "Lord, have mercy. Christ, have mercy."

One of them flicked water at Ben from a bowl. "I adjure you, every unclean spirit, every specter from hell, every satanic power, in the name of Jesus Christ of Nazareth, who was led into the desert after His baptism by John to vanquish you in your citadel, to cease your assaults against this creature whom He has formed from the slime of the Earth for His own honor and glory; to quail before wretched man, seeing in him the image of Almighty God rather than his state of human frailty. Yield then to God, who is His servant—"

Ben wrenched wildly against his restraints and kicked the bowl out of the priest's grip, showering Aiwass, who started to vibrate violently. His energy scattered around the room, reaching into every physical thing. The priests retreated in fear as the room began to warp and buzz threateningly.

Ben watched Aiwass rise above the dog, a swirling, golden ball of discarnate energy. *Marvelous. Now I am without a body yet again.*

"I didn't know you could do that!" Ben said.

I didn't do that quite on purpose. But watch this.

Aiwass floated into Ben's head, and suddenly his vision snapped to outside the room, where the priests stood arguing.

"How have we made this worse?" Raul asked the main

priest. "He's even more possessed than before! This is something more powerful than we have ever encountered."

"Do you think it's . . . ?"

"I definitely think his parents tried to call the moonchild into him. Did you see that glowing seal on his forehead? I don't think there's anything we can do."

"That settles it, then. We must kill him."

The priests began digging through chests, looking for something. They left the room through an adjacent hallway.

Ben snapped back to himself in a panic. "They want to kill me?"

Don't worry. I have another trick up my sleeve.

Aiwass moved into the restraints holding Ben's hands, and slowly the ropes loosened until Ben was able to pull his hands out.

"Wait, if you could do that all along, then why didn't you?"

If I had done that earlier, they would have caught you, and your death would have been guaranteed. Also, as you know, my spirit was previously bound to that dog.

Ben finished freeing himself and made a break for the door.

Pick up the dog.

"I thought you were the dog."

I inhabited the dog because there was nothing else available at the time. I need you to bring it if I am to have any chance of getting back into its body.

Ben picked up the puppy just as the priests returned. As he sprinted for the exit, he could hear them shouting, but he didn't stop. He ran as fast as he could, out of the church and into the street. He didn't stop until he was far away.

"What now? I can't go home. I—"

I know where we can go.

. . .

Ben stepped through the automatic doors of the large skyscraper. Inside was a lavish lobby with walls and floor overlaid in marble. A long, dark-red carpet flowed through the center of the room, leading from the entrance into the depths of the building. Hanging lights shaped like orbs cast shadows in all directions. A large reception desk stood to the left, and the total absence of people created an eerie ambience. Aiwass floated next to Ben, his soft golden glow adding to the insidious atmosphere.

"Are you sure we're in the right place?" Ben said.

I am sure.

"How? How can you be sure?" Ben's voice rose, echoing throughout the empty lobby.

No need to yell. As part of my ethereal abilities, I am able to read people's minds.

Ben stopped and looked at Aiwass. "You're kidding."

I am a discarnate ball of energy, and that is what you find unbelievable?

"Good point." Ben started walking again. "So, whose mind did you read?"

The priests'. They were afraid you would find this place, which made it simple for me to figure out where it was.

"Why would they be afraid of me finding this place? Unless . . . this is where I will finally open myself up and become illuminated."

Aiwass said nothing.

As Ben continued walking, he looked at the strange art that lined the walls. The images were a mix of abstract and symbolic designs, obviously created with a specific purpose in mind. "What do they mean?"

You don't recognize them?

"Why would I . . . ?" Ben's voice trailed off as he looked

closer. "You're right, some of these paintings are in my dad's house, too. But why would he have them?"

Isn't it obvious? Your father is part of this cult.

"Cult?"

What else would you call it?

Ben stood in silence looking at the sinister artwork.

This is exactly where we need to be to reverse what has been done to you, and to see if you can be illuminated.

Ben still carried the dog, but Aiwass was starting to revert into its body, and Ben could feel the puppy trying to wriggle free. When he put the dog down on the marble floor, Aiwass seemed to be in control of its movements.

Almost as if answering Ben's thoughts, Aiwass confirmed, *I am within the dog once more. The holy water they used wasn't very strong, so it didn't last long. Pathetic.*

Ben continued deeper into the lobby. Gradually, the room narrowed, and soon they were walking down a long hall with doors on either side. Ben peeked through a window set into one of the doors and saw a conference room with a large, oval table and chairs in the center. Monitors and other electronic equipment were embedded in the walls. It looked like the gear was designed for surveillance.

Ben reached the end of the long hallway. An elevator greeted them with a chime, and they stepped inside. "Where should we go now?"

Aiwass scratched his ear with his hind leg. After a moment, he stopped, and his eyes glowed orange. *To the top.*

The elevator arrived at the top floor. The number "33" glowed an ominous green from the display above the doors. The elevator opened, revealing a long, empty corridor that resembled the one they had already passed through.

Ben glanced over at Aiwass, who sat waiting for him with his tail between his legs. He stepped forward cautiously and made his way down the corridor until he heard people talking nearby. He knelt down and strained his ears to hear.

". . . and then what?" the first voice demanded. "Do you really think we can open the seal without—?"

"It is not your position to ask questions. Do not doubt the grand design of the prophecy. We must continue the rituals. All will work out as planned."

"But—"

"No buts. We missed our opportunity before, and we must not miss it again."

"That was eighteen years ago! We won't—"

"Exactly. Do you really want to wait another eighteen?"

Ben glanced at Aiwass, who was licking his genitals. "What are you doing?" he whispered harshly.

What? I'm a dog. Might as well act the part.

"What should we do?"

Aiwass stopped licking himself and edged slowly toward Ben. *We cannot allow them to complete the ritual, not yet.*

"Not yet?" Ben was incredulous.

No. Follow me.

With that, Aiwass trotted into the room, keeping to the shadows cast by the large, marble pillars. Ben followed cautiously. They snuck past several guards and around a corner. Ben looked into Aiwass' eyes and saw a faint glow in them that seemed to pulse brighter the closer they got to . . . something.

"Where are you leading me?"

The only way to reverse what has been done to you is to kill the leader of the cult.

"What?" Ben's heart jumped into his throat.

You want to reverse this, don't you? Aiwass stopped where

he was and looked back at Ben. His tongue poked out of his mouth, lightly panting as if from exertion. *Only then can you be illuminated.*

"Of course I do, but I don't want to kill someone."

You might not have a choice. Aiwass continued forward, and Ben hesitated for a moment before creeping after him.

They peered around a large door frame into a huge, open room. Several people wearing dark, hooded cloaks stood inside. They chanted as they stepped backward, creating a large circle. Ben couldn't see what was in the center of the circle.

He glanced at Aiwass, but before he could speak, a hand grabbed him from behind. He let out a grunt as he was pushed to the floor.

"Look what I found!" The voice was gravelly and deep.

Ben tried to look back to see who had caught him, but the hands held him tightly and yanked him to his feet. The others stopped what they were doing, and their demeanors changed immediately.

"Ah, just in time! We thought you might not make it. Quickly," one of the figures said as he lowered his hood to reveal balding gray hair, "bring him over here."

"No! Let go of me!" Ben struggled, to no avail. He looked around wildly and saw Aiwass skulking off into the shadows. "Stupid dog, get back here and help me!"

Do not worry for me. I will wait until the time is right, and then I will save the day—as always.

Ben was placed on the altar and held down while the other robed figures approached and looked him over. They terrified him. He couldn't make out their faces, only a darkness within their baggy hoods that seemed to envelop him.

"We must finish the ritual," someone said from behind him.

The words sent a chill up Ben's spine. He had no idea why Aiwass thought he would be able to kill the leader. All he could think of was how he might escape, but he couldn't wrench free of the hands holding him in place.

The old man moved in front of Ben and wiped some slimy liquid on his brow and cheeks. It reeked, and he scrunched his nose at the putrid smell.

"OMNACRA-ZOH-ES-AH!"

The words vibrated within Ben. He had heard them before; they were the same words his father had spoken. Now he knew with complete certainty that his father was connected to this group, just as Aiwass had said.

The old man lowered a jug to Ben's lips and grinned as he poured the rancid slime into the boy's mouth. At first, Ben gagged, but then he resigned himself to what was happening. There wasn't anything he could do. Or was there?

He held the liquid in his mouth until it spilled out over his face and down his shoulders. The hooded figures pulled the jug back and continued to chant. The old man held out his hand and sliced it with a knife, letting the blood drip onto Ben's forehead.

Ben had flashbacks to his father's ritual: the incandescent glow of the candles, the eerie chanting, the blood dripping on his skin. Looking out among the cloaked figures, he thought he spotted Anthony's face beneath a hood. He mustered up all his strength and spat the stinky slime into the eyes of the man holding him down.

The man gave a shrill scream of pain and let go of Ben. He managed to wriggle free from the others and jump up. The look in the old man's eyes showed confusion and shock. Out of nowhere, Aiwass leaped up and knocked the bewildered old man to the ground. Ben ran away as fast as he could with Aiwass at his side. Shouts chased him, but he refused to stop.

· · ·

Ben walked slowly down the street. It was now night, and he had nowhere to go. He worried about what to do next, but nothing seemed to bother Aiwass, who trotted beside him in his usual happy way.

Since Ben's father was connected to the cult, there was no way he could go back home. After encountering the priests, he was scared of what else might happen to him. He didn't know who to trust. Only Aiwass seemed to have his best interests at heart.

Ben stopped and sat down on the sidewalk. Aiwass curled up between his legs, his big puppy eyes gazing up at Ben. It was as if they pierced his soul.

"It's just you and me against the world." Ben looked down at the pavement and ran a hand through his hair.

We will survive. Don't worry your human brain.

Ben cuddled up to Aiwass, and the two fell asleep.

It was dark, and Ben couldn't see his hands in front of him. He didn't know where he was, but he felt comfort in the fact that Aiwass was there, even though he saw nothing.

A cold, burning sensation enveloped his stomach, and he began to panic. Reaching out, he waved his arms in front of him. He felt all around, but there was no road, no grass. What was he sitting on? Then he realized he wasn't sitting. There was literally nothing around him.

Aiwass's booming voice in his head gave him a fright. *Nothing can harm you here.*

Where are we?

We are neither physical nor mental. We are on an ethereal plane of emotional existence.

What are we doing here?

If we plan to escape from the cult as well as the priests, we need to pool our energies together.

How do we do that?

Do you trust me?

I do.

Watch.

With that, Ben sensed Aiwass' essence entering his body. It felt like a warm waterfall flowing in through the crown of his head. It swirled around inside him, welling up within his extremities and heating his whole body. Like a zap of lightning, he felt his body reanimate. He fell backward but didn't hit the ground. He plummeted into nothingness. The overwhelming feeling of falling enveloped him, and he returned to the black expanse of nothingness from whence he came.

Smoke swirled in the corners of Ben's vision. His body moved without any conscious thought on his part, as if it were no longer under his control. A conversation seemed to be going on nearby, but he couldn't tell who was talking.

"Did the ritual work?"

"It did. I am now sealed within Ben, and just in time. All I had to do was get him to trust me."

Ben felt the cold concrete floor beneath him. As his vision slowly returned, he could make out the eerie glow of candles. He was sitting in his father's basement. Had he ever left? He saw his reflection in the mirrors, but he didn't recognize himself. His eyes were a burning shade of amber. That stupid dog had betrayed him!

"The seal of manifestation is opening. I can feel it. Now it is time to complete our mission and release this energy on the world."

About the Author

Steven Dutch was born in Auckland, New Zealand but grew up in Sydney, Australia. He would consider himself a foodie, and enjoys most cultures foods. He works a day job as a Cyber Security Service Delivery Manager and enjoys everything scientific and technological, which bleeds over into his writing often. He has always been fascinated by science fiction and magic, thinking there is a fine line between the two and enjoys writing stories meshing and melding the two together. He has been writing for over 12 years and has completed several writing seminars and courses. He has written several short stories and working with Chris Masterton has written 3 Novellas in a science fiction series called History of Sol.

www.historyofsol.com

Warts and Wishes

A. A. WARNE

Gregory slid the small blood vial back onto the shelf and picked up the next one. He shook it several times until the discoloration evened out, then replaced it. Using a crooked walking stick to support his bad leg, he hobbled around the shop, shaking only the most valuable bottles of blood.

As soon as he sat back down on his stool, the little bell above the door chimed, announcing his first customer of the day.

"Mrs. Buckley!" he sang out politely, even as he refrained from rolling his eyes. This was her third visit this week. "What brings you in today?"

She dropped a soaked umbrella into the mosaic stand by the door, then unbuttoned her oversized red coat and flung it onto the black coatrack. In her epic dance of an entrance, she somehow managed to spray water across half the store, leaving a droplet sliding down Gregory's bald head.

"My son!" she cried, tucking her arms around the half-forgotten child beside her and pushing him toward the counter. "He woke up with warts."

Gregory eyed the boy, noting the size and placement of each raised wart. "Are you sure he didn't go to bed with them?"

She tsked. "Of course I'm sure."

Gregory pinched his chin, pulling on the hairs of his white beard. He usually considered all logical solutions before resorting to his special blood concoctions, particularly because he didn't want to run out of stock. "Is this the same child I provided the unicorn blood for last month?"

"Oh no, that was for my eldest son. Tristan is my second youngest."

"And the other six boys? All healthy and fine?"

She fussed over the boy, tucking a stray hair behind his ear, which was as rosy as his cheeks. "Not a wart in sight."

Turning his back, Gregory picked up a vial, felt its energy, and returned it to the shelf. Warts were often treated with fairy's blood, but whenever Gregory treated Mrs. Buckley's brood with conventional means, she always came back complaining of unusual symptoms.

Bloody difficult, that lot.

He had an idea. Tucked in the far back corner was a cheap bottle so old the blood had turned brown.

"Here we go. I have the perfect thing: bat's blood."

Her eyes went wide. "That's the cure?"

"I wouldn't recommend it if it wasn't," he said in a tone that suggested she shouldn't question his expertise further.

"And it's fresh? How do I use it?"

"All my products are fresh and cleansed. Just two drops under the tongue twice a day. I'll even give you a discount for being such a loyal customer." He winked, and she flashed her pearly white teeth.

As she retrieved the shillings from her purse, the bell chimed again. Gregory eyed the new customer, who was cloaked in darkness, hiding their face beneath a hood.

"You have a perfect weekend now, Mrs. Buckley." Gregory sat back on his stool and watched the figure move around the room while Mrs. Buckley gathered her things and went outside into the pouring rain.

As soon as the door closed, the figure pulled back its hood to reveal a bald head—a telltale sign that he too was a practitioner of the healing arts, or perhaps a con artist who was mimicking Gregory. The mysterious man approached the counter.

"What can I do for you?" Keeping his voice low and calm, Gregory breathed in the scents of wet cloth, starch, and something unusual that lay heavy on the man's breath.

"It's not what you can do for me, but what I can do for you."

"Get out. I don't deal with swindlers."

The man laughed, turned his head to the side, and rolled back the cartilage of his ear to display the sacred figure eight symbol. "Since when do swindlers get branded?"

Gregory sighed. "As you can see, I have more stock than I can sell. I'm not in the position to buy."

"You are well stocked. However, I hear this area needs more incentive for your services, so I come with a gift." He slipped a hand beneath his robe and pulled out a small pitcher, corked at the top. "Try this on your customers. If you're happy, I'll come back with more. I don't even want payment for the blood up front."

Gregory eyed the pitcher. It was an unusual shape, narrow at the top and swollen around the middle. He couldn't help but think that the earthenware had been bent out of its original shape. Reaching across the table, he pushed it back toward the mysterious stranger.

"I didn't ask for help," he said smoothly, "and there's the door."

"Like I said, it's a gift." The hood went up, and the man left Gregory's shop in a flash, like a wisp of smoke dissipating in the air.

Gregory sighed and shoved the pitcher beneath the counter.

"Mr. Gregory!" Mrs. Buckley rushed through the door with four of her boys in tow. "Please, Mr. Gregory!" she cried, not even taking off her coat as they approached the counter. "My son!"

Gregory hobbled in from the back, clipping his belt together. *For a dead-quiet store, I can't even take a piss.*

"Oh, thank the Lord you're here." Mrs. Buckley wiped tears from her eyes.

Sitting on his stool, he let out a heartfelt sigh. "Where else would I be?"

"Look at my son." She stepped aside to reveal the same boy from the previous visit. "The medicine didn't work!"

Gregory leaned over the counter, his full belly pressing uncomfortably against the wood. The sight of the boy stopped his breath. Warts covered him from head to toe until there was barely any soft skin left.

"My God!" He exhaled and clutched his chest. "When did this happen?"

"He woke up like that!"

"And you only gave him two drops?"

She nodded frantically.

Gregory collapsed on his stool, clearing his mind. "Don't touch that!" he snapped at the other boys, who were rummaging through his stock. They jumped, then put the vials back on the shelf.

Mrs. Buckley ordered the boys to her side. They were all reasonably well-behaved and did as they were told, but Gregory struggled to think as five sets of eyes stared at him.

"There's something new—"

She cut him off. "I'll try anything!"

He frowned. "That's what I'm worried about. They're only warts; they'll go away eventually. I don't even know the risks—"

She didn't let him finish. He bit his tongue and listened. "My poor son! He can't live like this. Please, I'm begging you. Help him."

Gregory closed his eyes and opened them again. "Fine, but he takes it here." He pulled the pitcher out from beneath the counter and shook it. "Get that stool," he said, pointing to the far back corner. "Pull him up closer. Boy, hold out your hand."

"Go on, Thomas. It's only medicine."

Gregory shivered. His blood wasn't medicine but rather a magical substance that enhanced the body's ability to heal itself. Blood for blood. Not everyone saw it the way he did, though, and most people either avoided the cobblestone street where his shop was located or threw rotten eggs at his door as they passed.

He pulled the cork lid off with a pop, and a faint blue puff of smoke came out. He fanned the smoke toward his face, inhaling deeply to inspect its aroma. Crimson iron was present, followed by a hidden wealth of lavender. Clearly, whatever beast the blood had come from, it had been fed well before it was bled.

"Now, son," Gregory said softly. He took the boy's hand and lowered a dropper into the container. "All actions of the body require intention. Today, we set the intention that this blood will cure your warts completely, never to return."

He released one drop, which landed on Thomas's wrist.

Instantly, the warts reduced in size, and within moments they were completely gone. Gregory's eyes went wide.

"Amazing!" Mrs. Buckley clapped her hands together, laughing with joy. "I knew you could do it."

Gregory inspected the boy's pupils and the whites of his eyes. When he pinched one of the child's fingertips, the skin turned white, then pink again as the blood returned. Satisfied with his cursory inspection of the boy's vitals, he asked, "Well, son, how do you feel?"

Thomas smiled. "I feel really good!"

Gregory placed a few more drops of blood on different parts of Thomas's body. It took only half of the small pitcher to cure the boy completely. "Did any of your other children catch the warts?"

"I didn't," the oldest spoke up, "but I want blue eyes." He reached for the dropper, snatching it out of Gregory's hands and wiping it over his eyelids.

"No!" Gregory cried. "This isn't to be trifled with."

The boy opened his eyes, which had become a sparkling blue.

"Oh, my." Mrs. Buckley stood back, taking in her son's new look. "How did it do that?"

Gregory marveled at the bottle. He was about to say, *I have no idea*, but he bit his tongue and decided to play the expert. "It's all about intention," he repeated.

"I'll take the rest of the bottle," she insisted. "Perhaps it will help my elderly mother. I will report back with the results." She dropped a full coin purse on the counter and scooped up the pitcher, disappearing out the door with her sons following close behind.

Standing there and taking in the moment, Gregory couldn't breathe. *Did that really happen?*

The next morning, Gregory looked out the window and spotted a familiar face he hadn't seen in years. "Margaret?"

"You old bastard!" She pushed her way in. "I sat in that bed for two years, and you didn't visit me once!"

Stumbling backward, Gregory pinched himself, convinced he was seeing a ghost.

"That blood you gave my daughter yesterday—I want more!"

"How are you even walking?"

She rolled her eyes and flicked up her wrinkled chin. "You were just waiting for my death notice, weren't you?"

"My dear Margaret," he said, holding the door open, "I would never wish such a thing on one of my best customers."

The years hadn't been kind to Margaret. A heavy smoker with a husky voice and a delicate frame, she had once been a baker's daughter who had elevated her station when she caught the eye of the local banker. She had borne him as many sons as she could, as well as a single daughter who had turned out to be just as annoying as Margaret herself.

"Now," she demanded, "where is it?"

He shrugged. "Sold out."

"Then get more!" She wrapped her scarf around her frail shoulders again. "Once everyone sees me, your little shop of bloody wonders will be packed for months."

Gregory felt sick. *What animal did that blood come from?* He paced the shop, quickly dealing with any customers who came in so he could return to his thoughts. By the end of the day, several new faces had popped in to put their name down on a waiting list. Since when did he have people waiting for blood?

He flipped the sign to show he was closed just as a knock came at the door. "Well, for the love of . . ." He sighed and cracked the door ajar. "Come back tomorrow. We're closed."

"Even for gifts?"

Gregory peered around the wooden frame and took in the hooded figure. "I have questions."

The mysterious man smiled. "Perhaps I can get out of the rain first?"

Opening the door wider, Gregory let him in, then locked up to prevent any interruptions. "Who are you?"

The stranger crossed the room, his gait awkward and stilted. He hoisted something up, and it banged on the top of the counter.

Gregory came closer, taking in the huge pitcher. It was the same color and shape as the first one, only far larger.

"What's this?"

"I said I'd return with another gift."

"Gift?" he yelled. "How can this be a gift? That must be five gallons of blood!"

"Eight, actually. That's why it's so hard to carry."

Gregory glared. "I don't want it."

The hooded man laughed. "You don't want to serve your customers and heal your community?"

The comment struck Gregory like a stab in the heart. He had sworn an oath, and his standing with the Ministry of Healing Arts would be jeopardized if he didn't uphold it. His duty was to serve the community and his brotherhood. To deny a branded brother would bring his own branding into question. "What sort of trickery is this?"

"Ah. I take it my gift was well received, then?" the stranger said with an amused grin.

Gregory aimed for his stool, desperate to get his weight off his failing legs. "I need to know what species it comes from."

"Under Section Three of the sacred oath and as your brother, I have given you a safe species."

"Then name it."

"If you are questioning my loyalty, I assure you this is not taboo blood."

Gregory opened a side drawer and retrieved a crystal wand. He only had five left, so he rarely used them. Taking the bottle of blood in one hand, he popped the cork, releasing the signature blue smoke.

"That," he said, pointing to the air, "I have not seen before."

"Part of the magic, wouldn't you say?"

Ignoring him, Gregory dipped the wand into the blood. Captured wands were valuable for three reasons: hunting desperate fairies, setting traps, and testing the purity of blood. If the wand turned black, it could mean only one thing: taboo.

"If you don't pull that out now, the blood will consume the wand."

"I like to make sure it's fully saturated so it gets a correct reading." Gregory smiled, flashing his stained teeth. He held it there a moment longer, then took it out and let it drip, inspecting the changes. He half-expected to see the wand turn dark, but instead it changed from a soft yellow to a sparkly purple so light it could be mistaken for white. "Interesting."

"Indeed," said the stranger. "This is my gift to you. After this, I will supply four large pitchers each month and receive sixty percent of the sale price in return. That's a nice profit for a quaint shop like this." He eyed the walls as if redecorating the place in his mind. He finally rested his gaze on Gregory again and extended a hand. "Do we have a deal?"

Gregory licked his lips and thought of ways to delay. There

was no denying the blood was potent. And the effects on Mrs. Buckley's mother, Margaret . . . How was that even possible?

Finally, he gave in despite his gut feeling, taking the man's hand and shaking it firmly. "We have a deal."

"See you in a month," the stranger said, and disappeared into the night.

By the time Gregory was halfway through the large pitcher of blood, word had spread to nearby towns. Travelers came for their own taste of healing, and his store was rarely empty. People no longer coughed, sickness had become part of the past, and workers churned out heavy workloads without tiring. Gregory didn't know what to think about it.

"Why haven't you taken any for your bad leg?" Mrs. Buckley said when she came in again, introducing more of her neighbors.

"The community always comes first," he said. "When there is an abundant supply, then I too will heal myself."

She smiled. "Oh, so noble, isn't he?" She winked to her neighbor, edging her forward for a purchase. Gregory had lost count of how many small vials he had given out at ridiculously high prices, but no one questioned the blood's worth. Some of the wealthier customers had even left hefty tips.

As he watched Mrs. Buckley leave, he wondered at how much had changed in a few days. She caught his stare and threw a smile over her shoulder. "I can just imagine the queen hearing about this and showing up here. They'll call it the Queen's Blood then."

The rest of the line cooed at the idea, and the whispers spread. "One vial of Queen's Blood, please?"

It was all they wanted, and they lined up in front of his

shop hours before he opened the door each morning. But before the entire pitcher was empty, everyone stopped coming. The streets were quiet, and no one left their homes.

Gregory stepped out into the street, expecting it to be full of busy people rushing in every direction, and saw nothing but cawing crows overhead. *Crows.* He hated that bad omen. Something was clearly wrong.

The crows squawked in unison, and every door along the cobblestone street opened at the same time. Blank faces appeared, and each person marched out of their home and began walking east one after another. Adults and children alike never blinked, never moved out of sync with one another. They walked past Gregory like he didn't exist.

"Stop!" he said to a man who wore a half-buttoned shirt over his pajama bottoms. The lids of his eyes were lifted so high his eyeballs protruded.

"I said stop!" Gregory yelled, but it was no use. Not a soul listened to him. They walked on in a daze.

Gregory hobbled back to his store, locking himself in. "Stupid! Stupid!" he cursed himself, rushing for the back of the store. He rummaged through old boxes, desperately searching for something he had hidden there long ago. Reaching down through the cobwebs and thick dust, he pulled out a tall, thin bottle. Its shape matched the figure eight brand behind his ear.

Rushing back to the counter, he placed his old walking stick on the stool, then held the vial in both hands. "I invoke the old gods to power this potion with strength and vitality. I reclaim all that has been given to me for the health and well-being of the community."

He pulled the wax seal off and popped the cork, gulping down half of the potion before pouring the rest over the stick. He coughed and struggled to keep the blood down. Although he wanted to remain upright to see the effects take hold, an intense pain spread from his chest out to his arms and collapsed his feeble old legs. All he remembered after that was the ground rushing up to meet him.

When Gregory opened his eyes, he sprang into action and got to his feet before he knew what he was doing. Looking down at himself, he saw that he was young again, his muscles strong and limber. He stretched and reached for his stick, only to find that it had transformed into the weapon he had once wielded before he became a master of the healing arts.

"Let's go," he said to his wooden sword, "we have a monster to kill."

Gregory slid the sword into his belt and rushed out into the crowd, quickly blending in with the rest. He had to blink every so often as his eyes dried out, but if he sensed anyone or anything watching, he endured the pain until the feeling passed.

He was the one who had given the insidious blood to his community, so he was the one who needed to save them. Never had he been so reckless and trusting before, even though he had not heard of a brother of the healing arts willing to cause such calamity in his lifetime. He just hoped there weren't any other brothers for him to deal with at the end of this march. One against one was a fair fight; two against one, and he was surely destined to lose.

Gregory flexed his young legs and felt the rejuvenated blood coursing through his body. He had taken the anti-aging potion twice in the past, extending his lifetime far beyond the norm, but he hadn't planned on doing it again until current events forced his hand. Whoever was looking for a fight had certainly picked the wrong old man to wrestle with.

The people in the crowd moved closer together as they marched, until they were bumping shoulders with one another. Gregory rushed forward, weaving between young and old alike as they continued mindlessly traveling toward an unknown destination. He shivered at the thought of what could have done this to them. Whatever it was, he would be ready, and so would his sword.

As the crowd approached the bridge, Gregory hoisted himself over the edge, lowering himself down onto the piers and jumping as far as possible to miss the water. By the time he crawled back up the ledge, the rain had started again.

Perfect, he thought, knowing that his movements would be covered by the sound. Using the trees as cover, he kept his distance and followed the crowd until it reached the end.

Every fiber in Gregory's body tensed when he spotted what awaited the victims. *It can't be!* There stood four figures: a blue genie, a siren, a vampire, and the mysterious man who had posed as a fellow brother of the healing arts. *An unholy alliance.*

The four mystical figures stood together like a team rather than the mortal enemies they were supposed to be. Everything became clear to Gregory now. The blood must have been a mix of the four, each component covering the others to avoid detection. But what Gregory couldn't work out was the why these beings would form such an alliance.

The people bowed before them. It didn't make sense. Genies served humanity, as did brothers of the healing arts. Vampires fed from humans, and sirens lured them in. But to force these people into servitude? It was beyond Gregory.

He gulped as a knife pressed against his throat.

"Move, and you die." He froze and did as he was told. "Now turn around slowly."

He pushed himself up and turned to face his enemy. Two orange, glowing eyes glared back at him. *A demon.*

"You have served me well. If I didn't plan on killing you, you would be a valuable asset in my ranks."

Clearly, the demon had more powers than Gregory could comprehend. As they circled one another, he tried to find a weakness in the demon's stance. "You recognize me?"

The demon lifted a leather-skinned eyebrow. "I see souls, not the perishable form you have used to disguise yourself. Why do you hide, brother?"

"I am no relation of yours."

The demon leaned back and let out a loud belly laugh. As though in sync with the demon, the people in the crowd laughed, too. "But you are!" It calmed down, breathing in deeply. "You and I are the same, with but one difference."

"Conviction?"

"Denial of oneself." The demon stepped to the side, waving its hand over the crowd. "You serve these slaves, and yet they are here to serve you."

"They are not slaves! That's not how this world works!"

The demon stomped its foot. The ground rumbled. "You were given this region, and it was you alone who spoiled it."

Gregory bit his lip. He was oath-sworn and had never swayed from his duty. "I will make this right. On my watch, this region has always been pure in its form!" He pulled out his sword, and it glowed bright-blue, releasing sparks of lightning. "And it will remain pure."

"You are no longer in control. This region is now mine!"

"Over my dead body!"

The demon smiled, showing its sharp, white teeth. "Exact-ly." It slammed its foot down again, and the earth started to shake.

Gregory stood firmly, and once the ground stopped heaving, he stomped his own foot. The soil softened beneath their feet, first rolling up like a carpet, then lifting to form walls, enclosing them within a roofless cavern.

"Your tricks won't save your world," the demon taunted.

"I have no tricks, but I will protect this world against your tyranny and poison." He held the sword up to the sky. Lightning struck it, illuminating its edges.

The demon leaned back and laughed again. Before the sword had absorbed enough energy, Gregory directed the lightning straight for its evil heart. The demon sidestepped the attack, rushing at him and clamping its hands around Gregory's neck.

"Give up now, and I'll let you join the peasants."

Gregory slid out of its hold, using the sword's charge to burn the demon's skin.

"You don't recognize me, do you, brother?"

"I am *not* your brother," Gregory spat.

"We are of the same blood. Has this world truly unhinged your brain?"

Gregory glared into the orange eyes and saw that the demon had no soul. "You cannot have brothers, so stop calling me that!"

They circled one another until the demon launched forward, smashing Gregory's jaw with its fist. Three, four, then a dozen times the demon struck him, until Gregory's legs buckled and he collapsed. "I told you to give up!"

Gregory's eyes rolled back, lids closing involuntarily as darkness loomed at the edges of his sight. He had the demon right where he wanted it.

The sword slipped from Gregory's hand. The demon watched the sparks fizzle out as it turned back to wood and clattered to the ground. Victory in sight, the demon leaned over Gregory, baring its teeth in a vicious grin. "I told you . . ."

The demon stopped, eyes wide, and shrieked. In its belly was a small blade dipped in Gregory's purest sample of blood. The potion was a remarkable remedy for infertility but sheer poison to a demon.

The demon froze. People in the distance started screaming. The siren bellowed. Birds took off. Trees swayed. The demon let out a breath so dark it looked as though it were tainted with the genie's blue smoke.

Gregory clutched for the sword, and lightning instantly reenergized it. He cut through the demon, slicing the air to prevent the wisp of its essence from escaping and finding another body to consume.

Finally free, Gregory rolled over and gasped. Gulping in a deep breath, he wiped his face, realizing he was covered in a thick layer of black blood. He rolled over onto his hands and knees and crawled back into the forest.

People were running back toward town and hiding behind trees, some even grabbing sticks for makeshift weapons. The vampire dashed around, snapping necks. The genie twirled high above the trees, raining blue dust on the villagers and paralyzing them where they stood.

Gregory wiped his face again. The black blood oozed. "Stop!" he screamed.

The monsters turned to him. A piercing squeal filled the air, and Gregory covered his ears. His sword dangled from his hand. Then a swish of air rushed up behind him. He lowered his hands to take in the sound and swung around, ready to lash out against any attacker. The sword flickered with vibrant colors and searing red flames. He jabbed it forward but paused before striking his target.

The beautiful, long-haired siren stood in the demon's black blood. She dropped to her knees, threading her long fingers into the soil and keening sorrowfully.

Gregory eyed the area, searching for the demon's body, but all that remained was a dark puff of smoke and smudged dirt. "Who is the leader now?" he demanded.

The demon's ranking followers appeared around him,

snarling their threats, inching forward. He sensed nothing but death from them.

"I have a deal to make." Gregory stood firmly, locking eyes with each of them.

"You are in no position to make any deals," the vampire snarled.

Gregory tilted back his head and let out a heartfelt laugh. Internally, his guts writhed with such intense nausea he thought he might spew them out, but he couldn't let his enemies see that. Instead, he stood tall, squaring his shoulders and projecting as much false confidence into his voice as he could muster. "Were you not the ones who came into my shop to bargain with me?"

They eyed one another, each one clearly hoping that someone else would take the lead.

Before one of them took the chance, Gregory sucked in a breath and announced his offer. "Leave now and never return, and I will let you live."

"That's a deal?" the vampire scoffed.

"Is your life not worth it?" Gregory stifled another laugh.

The vampire's nostrils flared, and Gregory readied himself for a fight. But all four of the demon's followers simply bowed their heads in defeat.

The siren stood up, a clump of blood-saturated dirt in her hands. She looked utterly defeated by grief. "We accept the deal."

Gregory's heart sank as he realized they weren't the demon's followers—they were its lovers. They had devoted their souls to a soulless being. He couldn't let them leave and find another one to bind themselves to. The horrors they could unleash on the world would be blood on his hands.

Slowly, they backed away, putting more space between him

and them. Every muscle in Gregory's body zinged with anticipation. He had made the wrong choice, and he knew it.

Just as they turned their backs to leave, Gregory lifted his
sword and pointed it at them. They froze in place, unable to
move. The sword's electrical energy pulsated, dragging them
back toward him. He yanked the sword downward, forcing
them to jump back and land atop the demon's blood.

"I demand you stop!" the vampire said.

The siren sucked in a breath and screamed out a howl, but
it went straight past Gregory, missing him entirely. Unwilling
to let this go on any longer, Gregory lifted his sword to the sky
and asked for guidance. A twirl of violent air tunneled down
from the clouds, locking onto the trapped bodies.

The vampire tried to fight back, but its strength was no
match. The genie puffed out a burst of blue smoke, but again it
proved useless against the natural power of the old gods. The
siren screamed louder.

Gregory smirked, knowing the gods would come down any
minute to claim these wicked creatures. And yet for some
reason, the gods delayed their punishment. The siren's screams
began to pierce the tornado. The villagers who had been frozen
in place moments ago now rushed at Gregory, attacking with
their makeshift weapons.

"No!" he cried, lifting a hand to defend himself. He couldn't
fight back because he was bound by oath to protect them.

The siren's scream continued to rise, and more of his
community appeared, charging violently at him. He accepted
the beatings, concentrating on holding onto his sword so the
four powerful creatures never had a moment's freedom. The
people hit and scratched, kicked and charged. He accepted it
all as his punishment for harming them in the first place.

Suddenly, a flood of divine light shone over all the land.

The tornado disappeared, along with the unholy alliance. Gregory collapsed on the ground. Freed from enchantment, the people stood inspecting their new surroundings.

Mrs. Buckley rushed over, kneeling beside him. "Take this!" she cried, pulling a small vial from her top pocket.

It was the poisonous concoction that had caused this mess in the first place. He took the vial from her and threw it at the nearest tree. It smashed, coating the bark. Instantly, the tree leaves wilted and fell. The branches flopped, and the tree darkened as though it were slowly turning to ash.

"Never again," Gregory whispered.

"But without the potion, you'll die!"

He smiled. "I have already lived too many lives. If I am meant to live any more, then let my body repair itself." And with that, he closed his eyes.

About the Author

A. A. Warne writes elaborate, strange, dark, and twisted stories. In other words, speculative fiction. Loacted at the bottom of the Blue Mountains in Sydney, Australia, Amanda was born an artist and grew up a painter before deciding to study pottery. But it wasn't until she found the art of the written word that her universe expanded. A graduate of Western Sydney University in Arts, Amanda now spends her time wrestling three kids and writing full time.

www.aawarne.com

Stupid Love

MADILYNN DALE

Harry rubbed his head as pressure pushed against his skull. The light from the computer strained his eyes, and his head throbbed. He stared at the spell, squinting as he wondered whether or not it would work.

He stood and paced around the room, running his hands through his hair. Hours had slipped by in his frantic search. He sat down again and scrolled through several more articles, but found himself going back to the first.

Looking at the fine print, Harry pursed his lips. A spell to save another requires great sacrifice, but at least he had found the solution to his wife's Stage IV cancer. He did a victory dance in his office chair, fist pumping the air. Shifting his weight to revive his sleeping muscles, he hit print and darted to the printer. He wrung his hands, sweat beading on his brow as the printer slowly spat out the paper.

April's faint snores and the thrumming of medical machinery broke the silence of the night. He had everything to lose in performing this ritual. Any form of magic or witchcraft was frowned upon in his community. He had a reputation to uphold, but he was desperate. April was his life, his everything.

He grabbed the papers from the printer and scanned through the instructions. His heartbeat increased. Some items would have to be improvised, but he needed to complete the ritual tonight. Time was not on his side. Who cared if he wasn't an actual witch? He remembered his grandparents talking about the witches who had been in their family long ago, so it was in his blood. It had to work.

It took an hour to gather supplies from around the house, but Harry did his best to keep from making too much noise. April needed her sleep. He placed everything into a plastic bag and checked on her one more time before stepping into the night. Closing the door behind him, he smiled eagerly. His palms grew sweaty, and he stumbled across the lawn. The new moon shining overhead made him feel as if he were in a fantasy movie. A light fog hovered over the grass, creating a glaze of dew. He smelled the neighbors' laundry as the light breeze carried its scent from the clothesline in the next yard.

Setting the bag in the middle of the lawn, he reviewed the instructions on the page, which said to make three circles with salt. Harry shoved the instructions into his pocket, then formed the circles with shaky hands, starting with the largest before making a smaller one inside it, followed by another even smaller one in the center. After he completed the final circle, he set the container of salt on the ground and stepped forward.

Pulling out the folded sheet of paper from his back pocket, he dropped to his knees and closed his eyes. Breathing in and out calmed his mind. He licked his lips, trying but failing to combat his dry mouth. Opening his eyes, he focused his attention on the two candles, cup, lighter, and pocketknife before him. Using the lighter to ignite both candles, he began to chant softly.

. . .

I call to thee, one in the dark,
to grant this favor of my heart.
Hear my call, hear my plea,
darkened one, I summon thee.

Harry repeated the words as he picked up the knife and brought it to his hand. He sliced his palm and held it above the cup, grimacing at the pain. The sensation grew to a burn as blood dripped from his palm. The wind picked up and swirled around him, but only within the circles, as if the world outside remained untouched. Shaking his head, he focused all of his attention on the ritual.

The cup vibrated, and a misty, purple vortex sprang from inside. Harry dropped the knife, which landed beside him in the grass. Every muscle in his body quivered and his hair stood on end.

A humanoid figure appeared in the dark vortex and began to grow. Hands appeared first, then arms, feet, and legs. Its form solidified more as the ground began to quake, and a female figure stepped out of the mist.

The entity was gorgeous, with long, silver hair that fell past her waist. She appeared shapely but thin, with bright-red eyes and long arms that ended in black nails. Her mouth was set in an annoyed scowl. As Harry stared, two swirling black holes formed in the air, pulling in what little light was available as a pair of curling, obsidian horns materialized on her head. Harry faltered, crawling backward to the edge of the salt circle.

The demoness glanced around curiously before letting her gaze rest on him. "Who dares disturb Lia Lilim, daughter of Lilith?"

Harry gulped, resisting the urge to urinate in his terror. He had to do this. Thinking of April, he steeled himself and called forth what courage he could. "I called, mighty demoness, for aid."

Lia lifted her brow as she stared him down. "What aid do you seek from a demoness such as I?"

Harry glanced up at her, his anxiety growing. He forced himself to say, "I want my wife to be healed. She is the love of my life, but she has Stage IV brain cancer. Please take her cancer away so we can grow old together."

The demoness growled, and the ground around them shook again. "To do that, you must make a deal with me. I do not do such things for free. There must be a sacrifice or an exchange."

"I've very little left to give other than myself," Harry stated. "What would you want from me?"

The demoness chuckled. "A deal in blood and your ability to express emotion."

Harry paused, considering her words. It seemed straightforward, and she had said "express emotion," not "feel." He would still love April, and she would still love him. "I accept your terms, demoness."

Lia's face broke into a grin so wide and terrifying it reminded him of an evil Cheshire cat. "Good. Give me your hand."

Lia reached forward and grabbed his arm before he could move. She pressed her index finger into his wounded palm. Harry's vision wavered as she dug her nail into the gash. Blood poured from his palm and pain coursed down his arm. Fire swept through him, searing through every nerve. He opened his mouth but was unable to scream. As the pain receded, he felt cold dread replace it.

"The deal is done. Your wife's cancer is gone," Lia

announced, dropping Harry's hand as if it disgusted her. Then, with a snap of her fingers, she vanished.

Harry stared at the place where the demoness had stood. His head ached, and tangled emotions swirled within him. He remained kneeling in the circles for a moment longer, organizing his thoughts before kicking the salt across the grass. He blew out the candles and gathered his items. The task was complete, and his limbs felt heavy. Had it worked?

With all the items in hand, he returned to the house. His wife's monitors continued to hum, and he poked his head in briefly before retiring to the guest bedroom, where he had slept ever since April had been brought home on hospice care. He quickly fell into a deep sleep atop the comforter.

The next morning, Harry awoke to his wife yelling his name. His heart pounded, and it took a moment before her words registered. "Harry, call my doctor! Something's wrong!"

Harry rolled off the guest bed and dashed down the hall. He was still wearing yesterday's clothes, and his brain struggled to catch up with what was happening.

"What is it? What can I do?" He glanced around the room, bleary-eyed and still in a fog. Everything seemed the same as the day before.

April was sitting upright in bed, one thin hand probing her head. Her nightgown pooled around her hips. Worry was written across her face in a deep frown, and goosebumps covered her arms. "The tumor feels strange. I feel so weird, different from last night."

Harry blinked. Chills danced up and down his spine at the memory of what he had done. He pulled out his phone and scrolled to the doctor's number.

Dr. George answered right away. "Hello?"

"Hey, Doc, this is Harry Cordova. April is experiencing some strange sensations. Can we come in for a checkup?"

The line went silent for a moment. "Yes, but go to the ER first for some tests. I'll have them sent to my office and call you. I'll let Tricia know, and we can make room in the schedule."

"Thanks, Doc. We'll see you soon." Harry hung up and glanced at his wife. "Let's get you dressed."

Several hours later, following an MRI and blood work, April and Harry waited in a cold room surrounded by sterile objects. April sat in her wheelchair, frowning as she hummed to herself.

Harry scratched his chin. "Are you okay?"

April nodded. "I think so." She furrowed her brow and pursed her lips. "It's just strange."

"What's strange, love?"

April pushed a stray hair out of her eyes. "I have so much more energy today. I can't remember the last time I felt like this." She smiled and laughed as tears gathered in her eyes.

Harry studied her closely, wondering if the deal had worked. At least she seemed happy and full of energy.

They both snapped their attention to the door when it opened. Dr. George walked in, a stern expression on his face. He fiddled with the stack of papers in his hand before setting them down on the counter and washing his hands. He seemed anxious.

Dr. George dried his hands quickly. "I can't believe the MRI results. The blood work agrees with it, but I don't understand. Mr. and Mrs. Cordova, by some miracle, the brain tumor has vanished. Of course, I would like to keep an eye on Mrs. Cordova and have her come in for more testing in a couple of weeks, but it seems she is cancer free." He shrugged, looking perplexed.

Harry saw excitement and wonder dance across his wife's face. He, too, was excited, but his face felt tight, almost as if someone had injected him with Botox.

"Aren't you happy, Harry? I'm cancer free!" April exclaimed, staring hard at her husband.

"Of course I'm happy, April. How could I not be? The cancer is gone, and you get to live." Harry tried to smile. His cheeks twitched, but his face wouldn't budge. It only itched.

Harry watched as April's expression changed. She knit her brows together before turning back to Dr. George.

The doctor cleared his throat. "Well, I'll let you two go out and celebrate. My office will call later this week to arrange for someone to pick up the medical equipment you no longer need. I want to see you in three weeks, so stop at the front desk to schedule another appointment."

"Of course. Thank you, Doctor." Harry reached out to shake Dr. George's hand before turning to April. "Shall we?"

April nodded, and Harry walked behind her wheelchair. He stopped, ready to push her forward, but she shook her head.

"I think I can walk," April said as she pushed up from the chair. She wobbled on her feet momentarily before turning to offer her husband a bright smile.

They walked out of the room together, leaving the rented wheelchair behind. Dr. George's excited applause followed them down the hall. Harry, feeling April's strong grip, tried to smile, but his face tightened again. He felt at ease and his hands tingled, but his inner emotions refused to be expressed. The blood deal had worked!

His thoughts turned dark, however, when he thought of April questioning his joy. How could she question it? For years, he'd been hoping for her to be healed, and he had risked everything to make it happen. Maybe the change in her health would make her forget about his lack of expression. Her life was now hers to live.

Harry felt happy and light as he headed downtown in his car, old brick buildings flying by in a blur. He pulled into a waterfront parking lot at Luke's Bar and Grill, a local pub he had frequented in his younger years. He glanced around as he entered the building, then grabbed a chair next to his old friend Maverick. They were meeting to have a beer and enjoy the baseball game.

"Hey, man!" Harry shook his friend's hand.

Maverick smiled as he pulled his hand away and took a sip of beer. "How long has it been, buddy?"

The two men had been best friends since grade school, and Maverick had even been best man at Harry's wedding. Their friendship had been put on the back burner after April's cancer worsened, but that life seemed so long ago now. The last six months had gone by in the blink of an eye.

"Too long. Did you see that April's a bestseller now? Her book skyrocketed after it dropped."

"I did! That's amazing. Aren't you excited for her?" Maverick asked, taking another swig. The Dodgers played on the screen behind him.

Harry nodded. "I am."

Maverick frowned and set down his pint glass. "You don't seem like it. Your face hasn't changed at all in the few minutes we've been together."

Harry sighed. "Yeah, I know. It's hard to explain."

Maverick lifted his brow. "What do you mean, it's hard to explain? You have plenty to be happy about now. Not only do you have more freedom, but April is better, too."

Harry grabbed his beer and took a big drink. Life had been different since the cancer had disappeared. On the one hand, he enjoyed seeing his wife dive into her work and engage in her new passions, but on the other, he felt like distance had grown between them. It was because of the deal, of course, but he hadn't found a way around it yet.

As he set the bottle down, he looked at his friend. "I did something risky, and the consequences have made life a bit challenging."

Maverick tilted his head. "What exactly did you do?"

"You probably won't believe this, but I made a deal with a demon to heal April. In exchange, she took away my ability to express emotion. Honestly, it could have been worse."

"What do you mean, you made a deal with a demon? You can't be serious! How does that even work?"

Harry blew out a deep breath, wishing he could frown. "I summoned a demoness and asked for help. I made a deal in blood, and I'm lucky it didn't cost me my life."

"How exactly did you summon said demon?"

Harry wanted to scream at his friend. How could Maverick not believe him? "Look, I love April. I would've done anything to help her, even selling my left kidney. Instead, I did some digging into my ancestry and discovered that my great-great-grandmother was burned at the stake for practicing witchcraft. I thought I might be able to channel her power, so I found a ritual online and tried it out."

Harry's stomach knotted as anxiety reared its head. He had been trying to ignore the possibility that he'd made a mistake by bargaining with Lia. That was why he had avoided mentioning it to April so far.

Maverick frowned as he cast his gaze around the room. "That's insane. It really worked?"

"Of course it worked. April was cured, and she's been plugging away at her writing. Now we get to live our lives together until we die at an old age."

Maverick scratched his head. "That sounds wonderful. So nothing else has happened? There weren't any consequences?"

"That's what's making me paranoid. I haven't come across anything yet. I mean, I feel like there's a gap building between April and I, but we'll work it out. That's what couples do. I'm hoping to eventually find a way around the deal so I can express emotions again, but so far I've got *nada*."

Maverick picked up his glass and took a hearty swig as he scanned the room. His eyes widened. "Wait a minute, isn't that April over there? Who is she with? I've never seen him before."

Harry turned and gazed across the room. At first, he only saw a slender blonde kissing a man with black hair. Then the woman leaned back to grab something off the floor—a purse. When she sat up, her face turned briefly toward the bar. It was April. Harry let out a gasp and whipped back around. His heart jumped to his throat, and he felt sick.

"She's having an affair?" Harry looked at his friend, his chest tightening and vision blurring. "Did you know?"

Maverick shook his head. "I just said I've never seen him. Are you going over there?"

Harry looked down at his beer, wishing he could frown. His blood boiled. April was supposed to be working on her book series. *How could she do this to me? I sacrificed for her, and we've been together for years. How could she betray me?* His throat ached as he vacillated between disbelief, hurt, and rage.

Maverick flagged the waitress down. "We're going to need something stronger over here."

She nodded and quickly returned with their alcohol. Harry took the shot glass from the waitress before it even hit the table and downed it. He needed the liquid courage for what he planned to do. He pushed away from the table roughly and strode across the room to confront his wife. Butterflies warred against the anger and nausea churning in his stomach. His body grew hot as he quickly thought over the last six months, looking for something he had missed. When had this started?

He watched April as his steps took him closer, and her eyes widened when she met his gaze. His hands shook and sweat beaded on his lower back while his heart rate spiked. "April, how lovely to see you here. Introduce me to your friend, love?"

April's mouth gaped like a fish fighting for its life. "Oh, um . . . Harry, this is an old friend of mine, Jeremy."

Rage simmered in Harry, and his face itched as he tried but failed to show that anger. "Nice to meet you, Jeremy."

As Jeremy reached out to shake his hand, Harry swung his fist at the other man and knocked him from his chair. "Stay away from my wife!"

"Harry!" April shrieked. "What was that for?"

"You know why, April. How *could* you?"

"No, I don't! This is the most emotion you've shown since I've healed. Why did you hit him?"

"Because you're cheating on me! Don't think I missed that kiss!"

Jeremy pushed himself up off the ground and shoved Harry. "You really want to do this, old man? I've been giving her the love she needs."

Harry's stomach tightened. "Is this what you really want, April? I've spent every day devoting my life to you!"

"You did, yes, but then you changed. Sometimes I think you were happier when I was dying! I miss the man I fell in love with, but you're not him anymore!" April grabbed her purse, visibly upset.

Harry turned away and stomped back to his table. He glanced over his shoulder and spotted April running from the room. He'd deal more with her betrayal later.

Another shot of whiskey rested on the table when Harry returned to his chair, and Maverick pushed it toward him. "Well, that was intense. Do you think you got your point across?"

Harry nodded, silently swirling his drink around before chugging it. The liquid burned as it went down. "Thanks, man. I didn't expect this to happen. I don't know what to do."

"If you need a place to stay, my guest room is always open."

"Thanks. I know this is a lot for you, especially since we haven't spent much time together over the last few years."

Maverick chuckled. "You've had your hands full. You gave every spare moment of your time to April, and this is what she's doing in return? Besides, I'll always be here for you. You're like family."

Harry signaled for another shot. "Yeah, I know. But it still means a lot to me."

They drank until the bar closed, then walked back to Maverick's place. Even though all Harry wanted to do was scream, cry, or hit something, he stumbled through the door and into Maverick's guest room. As he lay there staring at the ceiling, the world spun around him. It seemed fitting for the chaos April had brought into his life.

The following evening when April arrived home, Harry was seated at the dining table, staring into a glass of scotch. His face was unreadable, but a tense vibe hung over the room.

"Hey. How was your day?" she asked meekly, moving toward him.

Harry looked up at his wife of the last ten years. Her hands trembled, and a frown wrinkled her face. Tears started falling down her cheeks, streaking her mascara. "You would be dead if it wasn't for me."

April dropped into a chair next to him. "What?"

Harry let out a defeated sigh. "I saw you with that man, and it wrecked me. How long has it been going on?"

Her gaze darted away from him. "I'm sorry, Harry. It was a one-time thing. I made a mistake."

"Don't lie to me. How long has the affair been going on?" His heart thudded dully in his chest.

April sobbed, "I'm so sorry. It just happened. You haven't been attentive, and I felt like we'd lost our connection. You say you love me, but your expressions say something different. Jeremy is someone I was interested in before you and I started dating, and he just happened to walk back into my life, almost like fate. I'm sorry, Harry. I just can't live with someone who doesn't love me!"

"How can you say that? April, I love you!" Harry slammed a hand to his heart. "I summoned a damn demon to save you!" His voice rose.

"That's impossible. Is this what my illness did? It drove you mad?"

"It didn't drive me mad." His heart pounded, and he grew breathless.

Hands clenched at her sides, April pushed back her chair, knocking it to the floor. "I can't do this anymore. I want a divorce."

"You don't want me?" Harry stammered.

"I want to be free to pursue my passions. I've been given a second chance at life, and I don't want to waste it! I want to be loved!" April screamed at him, tears streaming down her face.

Stunned, Harry stared at her, expressionless. Bile rose in his throat, and he felt as if he were watching their fight from outside his body. Was this really happening?

April wiped away her tears. "Even now, you say you care, but you hardly flinched at my request. I'm going to stay with my sister until we can figure out what to do next. I can't live with you anymore. Even when we make love, it's so mechanical, like it's just a job to you. I can't live this way!"

Harry pulled himself together by pinching his arm. "No, I'll go. I just need to gather a few things first. Maverick offered me a room."

Harry stood and walked down the hall to pack a bag. On his way, he glanced down and saw the crumpled piece of paper from the ritual. Grabbing it, he smoothed it out and glanced over the instructions, then stuffed it in his pocket.

He entered the master bedroom he and April had shared, and his heart clenched at all the memories ruined by her betrayal. Closing his eyes, he forced a deep breath in and out before slinging clothes into his bag. He had an idea.

Harry found himself taking a glass of scotch from Maverick. He wasn't sure how he had ended up in his friend's kitchen, but here he was. Harry stared at the amber liquid briefly before he gulped it down and headed out to Maverick's backyard. It was time to follow through on the idea he'd had while packing. Maverick followed, still carrying his glass.

"I need you to stand back and stay out of the circles while I do this," Harry said as he pulled out the ritual items he had used before.

He began making the circles of salt as Maverick watched in concern. "Are you sure this is a good idea? Isn't this ritual what got you into this mess?"

"April is what got me into this mess. Just stay back."

"Harry, I really don't think this is a good idea. You're not even sober!"

"Cut the crap, Maverick. I know what I'm doing!" Harry paused and stared at his friend, willing his face to be stern, but once again it just itched.

He placed everything exactly as he had before and stepped back. Taking a deep breath, he did his best to calm himself and push down the pain of his wife's betrayal. After some deep breathing, he lit the candles, cut his hand, and began to chant.

I call to thee, one in the dark,
to grant this favor of my heart.
Hear my call, hear my plea,
darkened one, I summon thee.

The vortex appeared above the candles, but this time, Harry did not step back. He glanced briefly at his best friend, who stared wide-eyed and trembling. When Lia appeared, he heard Maverick swear.

"Mortal," she said, glaring at Harry. "Why have you called upon me again? I fulfilled my part of the pact."

Harry looked up and met the demoness's gaze. "I wish to make another deal. My wife has betrayed me and is leaving me for another man. I seek to undo our previous bargain."

Lia burst into laughter. Goosebumps sprouted on Harry's arms, but he remained where he stood. "I cannot. What's done is done."

Harry's anger surged as his body grew hot, and he clenched his fists, fighting the urge to pummel her. "I summoned you, and you will do my bidding."

Lia cocked her head, clearly amused at his words. "Let your

friend bear witness to this. I will neither undo nor alter our deal. You are wasting your time and angering me. How dare you act as if you control me? Your wife's soul was meant to leave this world, but you bargained for it in exchange for your ability to express emotion. The Fates are not pleased with me, for they wanted different payment. Now, I shall take from you what I should have in the beginning."

A purple fire burst into life within the inner circle. Harry shrieked as the flames covered him and burned his skin. Then, with a shrill scream, he disappeared.

Lia remained standing in the circle, smiling. She turned to meet Maverick's terrified gaze, and he held up his hands to appease her. "I will not harm you, mortal, but take note of what has happened. I deal only in blood, and no longer shall I let my time be wasted."

"You killed my friend!"

"I did. He got what he deserved. Now, do you wish to make a deal?"

Maverick shook his head, then paused, assessing the circles before him. Could she bring Harry back?

The demoness glared at Maverick. "I warned you not to waste my time."

Then, before Maverick could speak, she vanished. The paper with the ritual instructions turned to ash on the ground where Harry had stood.

About the Author

Madilynn Dale is an author, blogger, freelancer, reader, mother, outdoors enthusiast, wine lover, and over all creative. She's a host for several shows featured under Go Indie Now's wide umbrella, hosts a podcast channel of her own, and loves to travel. Madilynn enjoys chatting with creatives from all areas of the field and letting her viewers see the authentic side of each one of them.

All That's Left

DRAGONNESS WYVERNA

Talitha's little brother was dying. Jagoraim lay on the floor of their hovel, feverish and struggling to breathe. When he did get enough air, he coughed it back up with such ferocity that Tali feared his lungs would come spilling out. She dabbed his forehead with a wet cloth, desperate to cool him down.

The door burst open, rattling the cracked wooden dishes on the table and knocking over the wobbly stool. Her second brother, Etan, brushed back his shaggy, brown hair and shook his head. His brown eyes looked sad as he walked over to her. "The hag won't come. Said Jag's got the plague, that we're all dead and we don't know it yet."

Talitha clenched her fist. "It's not the plague," she said between gritted teeth. "It's just a fever. It killed Mom and Dad, and it's killing him! She doesn't *want* to save him."

Etan straightened. "Why wouldn't the hag want to save him? He's a kid. He hasn't done her any harm."

"Because we can't pay," Talitha spat, fighting back tears. "She'll let Jag die because we can't put a smashed piece of metal in her greedy palm." She wiped her eyes and sniffed, but she wouldn't grieve. Not yet. Jag was still alive, still fighting, and she would do everything she could to help him. She took another rag and wet it, passing it to Etan. "Here, keep him cool."

Etan began dabbing Jagoraim's face and neck. "Where are you going?"

"To get help."

"But no one will help us."

Talitha looked at him, the truth of her errand burning in her mouth, but she didn't dare tell him. She forced a smile. "I'll *make* them help us." She grabbed her hat, scarf, and coat, and hurried out into the cold of Agril.

It hadn't snowed yet, but autumn had done its work. The hills that had once rolled with green were now dull yellow, and the butterflies that had fluttered from flower to flower were gone. Talitha shivered and pulled her scarf tighter around her neck, blowing into her hands to keep them warm as she trudged up the dirt road.

You followed certain rules in Agril if you were smart. Parents drilled them into their children like scripture, and Talitha's parents hadn't been any different. Talitha repeated them in her mind now, twisting the iron ring on her finger.

Never leave the house without your iron.

Never walk the hills at twilight.

Never cross the Gaelite rings.

Never stray from the path.

Talitha picked at her chapping lips and looked around. She saw no one else on the road or the hills. She went to the border of the road, staring at the dying grass as she tried to work up her courage. Taking a deep breath, she squeezed her eyes shut and stepped off the road.

Nothing happened.

Talitha's shoulders sagged with relief, and she automatically twisted her iron ring again as she took off farther into the hills. Part of her knew that keeping to the road was simply a way to avoid the Gaelite rings and that nothing would happen when she stepped onto the grass, but the childhood terror plagued her. It didn't help that she *wanted* to find a Gaelite ring, *wanted* to find the people of Gael.

The Pale Ones.

The Shining Ones.

The Kindly Ones.

Talitha shuddered and rubbed her arms. Gaelites were anything but kindly.

Her feet stopped shy of a mushroom circle. She stared at the little toadstools, their colors eerily bright against the dead of winter. When she shivered this time, it had nothing to do with the chill.

"'Never walk the hills at twilight,'" Talitha murmured to herself. "'Never stray from the path. Never cross the Gaelite rings.'" She closed her eyes and stepped into the circle.

She noticed the warmth first, then the smell of flowers and the laughter rippling from nearby. She opened her eyes and looked around. The sky was bright and blue, flowers waved knee-high in the grass, and birds flew overhead to land in the nearby trees.

"Oh dear, oh dear," a smooth voice tsked behind her. "Looks like a little Agriline wandered from the path."

Talitha shoved her terror down to her depths as she turned to face the ethereal beauty behind her. It was a tall man, pale as pearls except for his gold eyes. His long, black hair nearly covered his pointed ears, and his tunic looked like silk. He smiled, revealing his perfect teeth. Talitha couldn't help but take a step back.

The Kindly One circled her, studying her drab clothes and dark hair. Talitha hunched her shoulders and lifted her scarf, hiding as much as she could inside it despite the warmth.

"What brings you to Gael, little Agriline?" the Kindly One asked.

"I-I've come to speak to the Boreon." She kept her eyes lowered.

"The Boreon?" The Kindly One laughed and tugged at her scarf. "You're a brave little one, aren't you? Coming here for an audience with the Boreon, all alone."

Tali put her hand on his wrist, smiling as she heard the hiss of her iron ring making contact with his skin. "Alone, but not unarmed."

He snarled and pulled away, his golden eyes flashing black as he glared at her.

Tali squared her shoulders and faced him, chin up. "Take me to the Boreon."

The Kindly One's snarl turned into a cruel smirk. "Very well. As you command, *my lady*. Right this way." He gestured forward and made a mocking half bow, leading Tali toward the hills.

The air smelled of honey and fresh bread, filling her with an alien sense of comfort, while the laughter and singing she heard on the breeze seemed to welcome her home. Everything was green and growing, bright and warm, and colorful wisps floated from flower to flower. This world was enchanting, and it terrified her.

The Kindly One took her to the source of the sounds and laughter. Faeries lounged in an open field, feasting on a springtime bounty of fruits and meats. Sprites fed delicacies to trolls, and pixies and elves lay in the grass while satyrs and dryads played lutes, lyres, and pipes as they danced around the party.

At the head of the clearing, shaded by a flowering tree, sat one of the most beautiful men Talitha had ever seen. Even sitting, he was tall, his long, blond hair crowned by a laurel wreath. The Boreon's elegant clothes fit his lithe body closely, all green and gold, cut like leaves with a spiked collar. His face was narrow and sharply designed, his cheeks dusted with flecks of gold. An ebony chalice balanced in his long fingers as he watched his court lounge and play. Small, black eyes flicked to Tali as she and the Kindly One drew near, boring into her.

Tali kept her eyes ahead, though she couldn't help but adjust her scarf around her chin.

The Kindly One offered a flourishing bow. "Great Boreon, this Agriline seeks an audience with your magnificence."

"Does she?" the Boreon asked, his bored tone not quite matching the glimmer in his black eyes. "And what, pray tell, does she want with me?"

Tali stepped forward. "It's my little brother, sir. He's dying. He's cold, and he can barely breathe! Please help him. Please."

"And," the Boreon asked, swirling the wine in his cup, "what will you give me in return?"

Talitha adjusted her scarf again, avoiding his gaze. Although faeries had been known to accept other forms of payment, making deals with them never ended well. But what choice did she have?

The Boreon's thin lips twisted into a smile. "I see. A little beggar crawling to the feast, pleading for scraps."

She clenched her jaw and stayed silent.

The Kindly One snickered.

The Boreon passed his goblet to him, then stood and approached Tali, taking her chin in his hand, examining her. He smirked when she pulled away, and took the edge of her scarf between his fingers. "I'll take this."

She didn't flinch as the coarse yarn dragged across her neck. "What do you want with it?"

"Nothing at all." He tossed the scarf to a satyr, then

plucked an acorn from the grass. Removing the acorn's cap, he filled the hollow nut with wine before capping it again. He then placed the acorn in the palm of Tali's hand. "Let your brother drink this, and he will be warm, and you will never hear him cough again."

She blinked at the little thing, stifling a sob of relief. "Thank you. Thank you!"

Clutching the acorn to her heart, she turned and fled, finding the Gaelite ring and diving back into the cold winter of Agril. She shivered as the wind struck her exposed neck and coughed as the bitter air chilled her lungs, but she kept running all the way back to the cottage.

"Tali!" Etan still knelt at Jag's side, trying to keep him comfortable despite his shivers. "Did you talk to the hag? Is she going to help?"

Talitha shook her head wordlessly, not daring to explain how she'd come by the cure. She pressed her hand to Jag's forehead, her heart aching for him.

Jag opened his eyes, his teeth chattering. "T-Tali. I-I-I'm so c-cold."

"I know. Here, drink this. It will make you better." She uncapped the acorn and tilted his head up, helping him drink.

Etan hovered at her shoulder, holding his breath as Jag coughed once, twice, then stilled. Tali grabbed Etan's hand, eyes wide as they waited. After what felt like ages during which their little brother lay far too still and every nightmare of losing him came back to them, he drew in a breath. Tali and Etan cried out in relief, and Tali hugged Jag so tightly he groaned in protest.

"Tali! Let go!"

Tali laughed. "Never. I'm never letting go again." She squeezed him again before releasing him, still laughing as Etan reached over and ruffled Jag's hair. Jag swatted at his hand and tried to get up, but Tali pushed him back down. "You're still resting. You're not going to get out of this bed until tomorrow."

"But I've been in bed all day!" Jag complained. "I want to get up!"

"No," Tali laughed. "But I'll tell you what: I'll make some nice, hot soup!"

"With bread?"

Tali exchanged a glance with Etan, then ruffled Jag's hair fondly. "We'll see. For now, soup."

Jag huffed good-naturedly and settled back in his bed, pulling the blankets close around his shoulders.

Tali hurried over to the fire and began working on the promised soup, thin though it would be. She raided their meager pantry, adding what she could to the broth. She or Etan would have to go out and try to scrounge up some meat tomorrow. Tali mentally went over her list of things to do to get them through the winter.

"I heard the hag telling another family that you should burn the clothes and blankets of sick people," Etan whispered to her. "Should we do that for Jag so he doesn't get sick again?"

"We can't afford new clothes or blankets," Tali replied quietly. "We'll just have to risk it." And pray that the fae magic kept him from contracting the sickness again, although she dared not say so aloud.

Jag was up and about the next day, though he didn't have the same strength as before the fever. Still, his eyes were bright, and he eagerly resumed his life. He played in the snow with the other children, the cold never touching him. He never got short of breath either, despite his weakness. It seemed strange, but Tali didn't intend to question it, so long as her brother lived.

When spring came, they spent more time outside in the

warming world, watching the flowers grow and finding edible buds to supplement their diet. Tali stayed close to Jag as they roamed the woods, pausing to let him rest whenever he needed to. She played it off as stopping to dig around for roots and tubers.

"I miss running," Jag said suddenly.

Tali looked at him, her fingers half-black as she worked to dig out a dandelion root. "Running?"

He nodded. "I can't run anymore. The fever took it away."

Tali came over to sit next to him. "What do you mean?"

"I mean it's too hard." He looked down at his hands and sniffled. "I can't make my legs go fast. Sometimes . . . sometimes I can't make my legs go at all. They just stop."

Tali hugged him. "I'm sorry, Jag. I'm so sorry."

He burrowed into her arms, holding her tight. "Sometimes, I-I think all of me is going to stop, and I won't be able to make me go again."

"That won't happen," Tali swore. "It won't. You're going to live a long, happy life. Now come on, let's go home. I think I have enough dandelions, don't you?" She helped him stand.

He leaned on her heavily, his steps slow and faltering, though his breathing remained steady. Tali didn't hurry him, juggling her dandelions in one arm as she guided him back home. Their rundown little cottage had just come into view when Jag collapsed.

"Jag?" Tali caught him as best she could, dropping the dandelions in favor of her brother. "Jag! Jag!" He didn't respond when she shook him, and she felt a sob claw its way from her throat.

Etan was on the road from the market, and as soon as he heard her calling, he dropped his bundle and ran to her. "What happened?"

"We were foraging in the woods, and he just collapsed."

She hovered as Etan took Jag from her arms and carried him into the cottage, laying him in bed. "He doesn't have a fever, and his breathing is fine. I don't know what happened!"

"Get the hag."

Tali huffed. "She wouldn't help when we knew what was wrong with him. What makes you think she'll help now?"

"Who else would give us the time of day?" Etan demanded. He ran a hand through his hair and blew out a shaky breath. "Look, I got a little money in the market doing odd jobs. Tell the hag we can pay her. She'll help then."

Tali took a deep breath and touched Jag's cheek, more than a little scared for him. "All right, I'll go talk to her. Your money's in the bag you dropped?"

"Yeah. And don't worry about Jag. I'll keep an eye on him." Etan pulled a stool beside the bed and sat down, preparing to keep vigil.

Tali hurried out of the hovel, grabbing Etan's abandoned bag and running down the path toward the hag's cottage. She rooted through the bag for anything she could use to barter, so distracted she didn't notice when she left the road. One moment, she was hurrying through the still-crisp air of spring, and the next, the air was warm and bright and summery.

Tali froze when she heard the lute and the singing. "Oh, no." She retraced her steps, looking frantically for the Gaelite ring she'd stepped in. There was no sign of a mushroom circle anywhere.

"Well, well, well. If it isn't the little beggar girl, come to my feast again."

Tali whirled, her heart leaping into her throat as she faced the Boreon. She remembered her manners just in time and bowed, hoping she hadn't offended him. "Apologies, great Boreon. I didn't mean to come here."

"Did you not?" He took her chin and raised her eyes. "Then why are you here, little beggar?"

She pulled away, fighting the urge to burn him with her iron. "I didn't come to beg. Not to you."

He laughed at her defiance. "I assume your precious brother is happy and well, then? Running around the fields like a little rabbit?"

The tone of his voice, his words, tripped something in Tali's mind. She glared at him, curling her fists. "You did something to him, didn't you? You planned this. What did you do?"

"I did what you asked. I gave him breath and warmth." He tilted his head, his black eyes glittering dangerously.

Tali took a deep breath to calm herself. "Well, I don't need your help. I have money. I'm going to the hag. She'll help him now."

"Money?" He laughed. "You have money, you say? Let me see this money."

Tali dug around in Etan's bag, fumbling for the money her brother had acquired and finding nothing. She upended the bag, and Etan's meager possessions spilled onto the ground. There was a crumbling piece of brown bread, two turnips, and a precious chunk of white cheese, but no money. Tali stared at the small feast, then bit back a frustrated sob.

She looked up at the Boreon and asked bitterly, "What do you want?"

He smirked. "I think the question, my dear beggar, is what do *you* want?"

She clenched her fists as she gathered her thoughts. She needed to find a way to keep the Boreon from messing up her bargain. "I want Jag to be strong. I want him to be fast. I want him to be able to jump and bend and play. Now, what do you want?"

He glanced down at her turnips and cheese and raised an

amused eyebrow. Then he took her hand, raising it so her dull iron ring caught the light dimly.

She pulled her hand away. "Gaelites can't touch iron. It burns them."

"I can touch iron." He took her hand again, this time covering her ring with his fingers. "It doesn't burn me."

She glared at him, hiding her terror with anger. The iron was supposed to protect her from the Gaelites, but if it couldn't protect her from *him*, what was the point? She twisted the ring from her finger and threw it at him. "Fine. Take it."

He laughed, brushing his fingers behind her ear and pulling another acorn out of thin air. "For you."

She stared at it suspiciously. "This will wake him up? Give him his strength back?"

"It will give you everything you asked for." He took a step back and vanished into the shadows of the tree.

Tali blinked in surprise, then swore when she realized she was back in Agril. She checked to make sure she still had Etan's satchel, oddly thankful that the treats he'd bought were back inside the bag. The acorn was a hard, cold ball in her hand, but she held onto it as she ran back to the hovel.

Etan stood when she entered. "Where's the hag?"

"I never reached her. The Boreon got me."

He swore. "How? Your iron . . ."

"It didn't work on him, but I was able to make another deal." She held out the acorn. "This will help Jag."

Etan scowled. "*Another* deal? Tali, we didn't have to deal with the Kindly Ones at all! The money—"

"Was gone. It was gone. I looked for it." She shook her head.

"Tali . . ."

"I didn't have a choice! He grabbed me on the path, and I . . ." She ran a hand through her hair. "I think whatever is wrong with Jag is Gaelite magic. The hag won't be able to do anything."

"So the Kindly Ones made him sick, and you had to go back to them to fix him?"

"Yes." Tali looked at the acorn, her insides twisting with guilt. "Etan, I didn't have a choice."

"I know. Once you get in bed with a Kindly One, they never let you go." He stepped aside and let her approach their brother. "What is this going to do to him?"

"I told them I wanted Jag to wake up, that I wanted him to be strong and fast and jump and bend and play." She met his eyes. "I think I covered everything."

"Sounds good enough, at least."

Tali tilted Jag's head forward, unscrewing the acorn's cap. She felt a wave of déjà vu as she carefully poured the drops into his mouth.

It didn't take as long for the magic to work this time. Jag gasped and shot up, brown eyes wide as he looked at his siblings. "Was I asleep?"

"Only for a little bit," Tali promised, hugging him again. "How do you feel?"

Jag grinned. "I feel good."

"Good!" She opened Etan's satchel. "Look what Etan brought."

"Cheese!" He reached greedily for the white wheel.

Etan grinned and plucked the treat from Tali's hands. "I was saving this for dinner."

"Can I have a piece now?" Jag begged. "Please?"

"Fine, you little brat." There was a slight laugh in Etan's words as he broke off a small piece and handed it to him. He and Tali went to the kitchen area to prepare their meal, relaxing back into the family routine.

Spring grew warm, flowers bloomed, and animals crept out

from their hibernation to explore the reborn world. Etan went to town every day to work, bringing back money that, meager as it was, was more than they had ever seen. Tali felt relieved that they could afford food, though she was careful not to over-spend, ferreting small amounts away in case of trouble.

The youngest of their family improved greatly, too. Jag's strength grew far beyond normal, as did his speed and agility. Tali would find him carrying an entire fallen tree out of the forest for firewood, or catching a rabbit in flight. It scared her, but she didn't dare show it, not until one summer day when Jag came into the house, dejected and sullen.

"Jag?" Tali went to him. "Jagoraim, what's wrong?"

"Am I a changeling?"

The question felt like a barb to her heart. She pulled him into a fierce embrace. "No. No, you're not a changeling. Who told you that?"

"Florence." He was limp in her arms. "I beat her horse in a race, and she called me a changeling. She said I'm a Gaelite, but I'm not, right? I'm an Agriline, like you and Etan."

"Yes, of course you're not Gaelite. You're human. I promise, Jag."

"Then why am I so much faster and stronger than everyone else? I could barely do anything after I got sick, but now I can do everything! Well, almost." Jag hunched. "Tali, what's happening to me?"

She cradled him, biting her lip as she tried to figure out how to tell him. Finally, she sighed and sat down with him. "Jag, when you were sick, no one would come to help us, so I went to the only ones who would give it."

Jag's eyes widened. "The Kindly Ones? But they're bad people!"

"I know. But"—she touched his cheek, a sob bubbling up in her throat—"we lost Mom and Dad. I couldn't lose you, too."

It was Jag's turn to hug her. "I'm here, Tali. I'm here."

"I know you are."

"What's going to happen to me? Am I going to turn into a Gaelite?"

"No." She faced him. "The Kindly Ones only did what I asked. I asked them to make you warm, to let you breathe, to make you fast and strong, and that's what you are. And you are *human*."

He sniffled and wiped his eyes. "The Kindly Ones don't help for free. What did you give them?"

"My scarf and my ring. Nothing too important. Now, let's not worry about the Kindly Ones anymore. Let's . . ." She looked around. "Let's get some laundry done. You can help me wring out the blankets." She pulled him to his feet with a smile. "Will you grab the basket for me?"

Jag nodded, visibly relieved to have something to do. He ran around the house in a blur, grabbing the blankets and dirty clothes, throwing them into the basket before Talitha had taken a step.

She laughed. "Look at you! See? You're amazing."

He beamed and bounced on his toes with pride. "I'll race you to the river."

"Fine, but if you win, you have to get started on the washing."

"Watch, I can balance it on my head and still beat you!" He placed the basket of clothes on his head and raced off, disappearing into the woods.

Tali laughed again and walked leisurely through the trees, letting her little brother work off some of his energy with the laundry. The sweet air relaxed her. She closed her eyes, letting the dappled sunlight warm her cheeks.

The peace ended abruptly with a scream. Tali's heart jumped to her throat and wedged itself there. She forced it back down and began to run, racing to the river, where she found a young girl fleeing from Jag's bleeding body. Tali let out a heart-wrenching wail and fell at her brother's side, at first taking his hand but then pressing her hands over the stab wound in his stomach.

"No, no, no, no! Jag!" she half-sobbed, half-screamed. "Jag!"

"Oh, dear," the Boreon's smooth voice intruded. "What has happened here?"

She glared at the Gaelite through her tears. "How could you? He's a child!"

The Boreon shook his head, his face a mask of sympathy and regret. "There is no creature more terrible than a scared human. The fault lies with your people, not mine."

Tali remembered the fleeing girl—she thought it might have been Florence—and knew he was right. She swallowed again, blinking back tears. "Can you save him?"

"It will cost."

"What do you want now?" Her voice turned shrill, and she covered her mouth, pulling herself under control. Her brother's blood stained her lips, and she had to fight the bile that rose from its iron taste. "I want my brother to be healthy and live a long life. I want him to grow into a man. I want him to live."

The Boreon bowed as he offered her the acorn. "Your wish is my command."

She started to take the nut, then hesitated, her fingers hovering over its brown cap. "What will it cost?"

"You."

"What?"

"You." He smiled, his chilly eyes glittering. "A life costs a life, and I need a queen."

She stared at him, mouth open. "You . . . you want *me*? But I'm just a peasant girl! I'm dirty and rough and *common*. I'm not a queen!"

"You are to me." He crouched beside her, still looming over her. "You've intrigued me, little beggar. If you want your brother to live, you will come with me to Gael and be my queen."

"Tormenting a little boy is *not* the way to propose."

"Give me your answer."

She glared at him, her heart racing. If she went to Gael, she knew the Boreon wouldn't just make her his queen, he would make her one of *them*. Her life as she knew it would be over. She would be trapped in Gael, craving only their food, their sunlight, their company. She would lose her love for her brothers and find pleasure only in tormenting the people of Agril. It would be worse than death.

A slight groan escaped from Jag's lips, and her heart almost snapped. She couldn't let him die. He still had so much life to live! He was just a child.

His life was worth hers.

Tali nodded once. "I'll be your queen."

The Boreon's smile was as triumphant as it was cold as he pulled out a familiar iron ring. "Tell me your name."

She swallowed. "Tali."

"Your *full* name."

"Talitha of Tassons."

The Boreon took her hand and spread her fingers. "I bind you, Talitha of Tassons, to me, the Boreon of Gael, to be my queen so long as your brother lives."

He slipped the ring over her finger, and something in her began to burn. She cried out in pain as the Boreon pressed the cold acorn into her palm. She could feel her humanity being eaten away by the iron that had once protected it, but she fought back, gritting her teeth as she bent over her brother.

She twisted the cap open and poured the small amount of liquid into Jag's open mouth. As she watched anxiously, the hole in his chest closed and the pain left his face. His brown eyes fluttered open, and she could only imagine how she looked with his blood staining her hands and mouth.

Still, she smiled to reassure him. "Hey, Jag. You okay?"

"Flo . . ." His voice was rough, his gaze still unfocused.

"Shh, shh. Don't talk, just listen. I have to go now."

"Go?"

"Yes, I have to go. But you'll be okay. You will. You're going to live, Jag. You're going to grow up and be a man, a man as good and strong as Dad. You'll help Etan, and you'll be fine."

"What about you?"

"I'll be fine, too." Blinking back tears, she kissed his forehead, trying not to grimace at the blood she left behind. "I promise. I just can't . . . I can't go home with you. I can't be with you and Etan anymore."

"Why not?"

Tears began to leak down her cheeks, but she still smiled for him. "Because . . . I love you. And I will always love you. And I love Etan, too."

The Boreon took her hand. "That is enough of a goodbye. It is time to go."

"Tali." Jag grabbed her skirt as she stood. "Tali, where are you going?"

She couldn't answer; the Boreon was pulling her away. "I love you, Jag. Tell Etan I love him, too. And tell him I'm sorry."

Jag dragged himself to his feet, reaching after her, but even with his speed, he couldn't catch them. "Tali! Tali, come back! Come back! Please! Please, I love you!"

The world shifted around her as she called, "I love you, too!" Then the Gaelite summer surrounded her, and her old life was gone.

About the Author

Dragonness Wyverna is always writing in one of her never-ending stack of notebooks or buried in her growing mountain of books. Her dog, Pippin, is a bit of a bitzer super-gaurd dog, accompanies her on her walks along the Maryland trails, listening to the ghostly whistle of distant train horns. Dragonness has been a wrangler of school-age children, a knife seller, and the voice on the telephone, but she keeps striving to forge her path in the literary world, writing the books and stories she loves.

www.blottedinksite.wordpress.com

Three Pints

VICTORIA YOUNG

A percussive cacophony poured into the taxi, swelling against Luka's ears. Sirens in the distance ebbed and flowed, coursing through his veins. High-heeled shoes trotted past the idling engines on Main Street as the crosswalk pulsed one hundred and sixty beats per minute. His hand lingered on the door handle as he imagined himself opening the door.

Home, thanks, he thought.

Instead, he put his earbuds in to block the sound, stepped out onto the pavement, and closed the door behind him.

"It's about time you got here," said a muffled voice.

The earbuds were good at blocking out chaotic noise, but also fairly decent at preventing annoying people from bothering him. This time, the annoying person was his brother, and there could be no ignoring him.

Kyle stepped out from behind a bus stop and bowed theatrically, one hand clasping a purple satin top hat to his chest, the other outstretched toward the gates behind him. "If Heaven's gates are pearly white, then Hell's are painted gold."

That was Kyle: always dramatic. It didn't help that he'd

gotten the lead in their senior play, nor did it make him any less embarrassing to be around.

Luka glanced at the gates. Kyle had a point. Thick, gold-plated wrought iron bars stretched upward toward sharp, ornamental finials. Luka had always thought this place looked and felt more like hell than a hospital.

"Oh, come on," said Kyle. "I'm only joking."

"Easy for you to say." Kyle hadn't spent half his life in and out of this place.

"Look," said Kyle, "I know you don't want to go back there, but that's why I'm here. We'll get you in there together. You know the facts. Three tiny, measly pints. That's all. And you could save *three* lives! You were given magic blood for a reason, brother."

"Magic blood," Luka scoffed. If he could count on one thing, it was that there was no such thing as magic.

Luka wasn't entirely sure what scared him most. The needle? He should be used to them by now. Or perhaps it was the building itself? When he was younger, every admission seemed to result in a week, or even a month more than what was promised. He probably *should* want to flee, for fear of being locked up. But then again, his blood was truly rare, and now that it'd been more than five years since his treatment ended, he could give back to people the way he himself had gotten help. He wanted to go in there, really. Well, sort of.

"Luka, the hero." Kyle did a playful dance.

Luka sighed. His brother was painfully optimistic and excruciatingly imaginative. Next, Kyle would make some stupid joke about teleporting the donation out of his body.

"*Accio* blood!" Kyle seemed to read Luka's mind. As expected, nothing happened.

"You're so predictable," said Luka, shrugging. "Anyway, so what's with the hat?"

"You like it?" Kyle hopped over some agapanthus into a garden bed. A large, convex mirror hung on a steel post. It was a little bit cloudy and covered in gum, but there were still a few bare patches which could be used to navigate the tight turn into the parking garage entrance. Kyle placed the hat upon his disheveled hair and gazed into the mirror, inspecting his bulbous, warped reflection. He adjusted the hat back and forth, then nodded, apparently satisfied.

"It looks ridiculous." Luka thought he resembled a drunk ringmaster who'd stumbled into the hall of mirrors.

"You need to be less serious," Kyle scoffed. "Where were you today, anyway?"

"Um . . ." Luka couldn't think of an excuse—at least, not one he wanted to give. He'd spent the day filling out a college application. It seemed stupid now.

Thankfully, his brother didn't press him. Instead, he turned and walked toward Locke's Lane.

Luka hesitated. The path along the parking garage road would take them to the main gate in three minutes. Locke's Lane added another six. He felt conflicted. Surely time mattered with this kind of thing.

In general, Kyle paid little attention to time. He was always late to arrive and late to leave for everything. For some reason, their parents and friends seemed to accept this without complaint. "He's an artist," people would say, "so it's expected." Really, though, Kyle was just nosy. He was always daydreaming, a pen in one hand and a notebook in the other, scribbling down conversations he overheard from strangers. Luka had tried many times to make him stop, but Kyle always shrugged and said the best stories stemmed from gossip, then kept on scribbling.

Luka wasn't particularly surprised by Kyle's decision to take the longer route. There was usually a group or two of people he could listen to on the way. But what did surprise him as he made his way down the cobblestone path was his own decision to follow his brother. Usually, Luka was an "arrive one minute early" kind of guy, so why did he want to go the long way today? He supposed his uneasiness about the destination made the journey more appealing.

A food truck was parked by the east entrance to the hospital grounds, so Locke's Lane was busier than usual. Workers and patients alike—some still in their slippers—stood alone or in huddles, drinking coffee and smoking cigarettes.

Luka wondered if they needed a sales rep. "Buy a coffee in the lane; it's twice the price of the cafeteria and comes with secondhand smoking!" He figured it probably wouldn't be their best marketing campaign.

"Oof!" Luka stumbled into Kyle's back, getting a mouthful of his scarf. "Were you always wearing that?" he asked as he picked green fibers from his teeth.

"Hmmm, maybe." Kyle wasn't listening. He wrote something in his notebook before he placed it in his coat pocket. "So, I was thinking . . ." Kyle turned to face him and took several steps back until he stood at the edge of the east gateway. "I said I'd help you, but first I'm going to make you a deal."

Luka's ears pricked. Once, he got to choose what their family played for game night five weeks in a row, all for the price of making his brother's bed on Sundays. Luka was so pleased with this deal that he also tried to throw in alphabetizing Kyle's books, but Kyle didn't go for it. He just didn't have the appreciation for cleanliness that Luka did. Still, it was a great deal, and the family played a lot of Monopoly that month. The joke was on Kyle, since Luka preferred to keep their shared room tidy anyway.

"What's the deal?" Luka asked.

"Well, I'm only going to help you get in there if you listen to me."

"I do listen to you."

"No, you don't. Not really. You listen, but you don't *hear* me."

Luka didn't understand. Was there a difference?

Kyle continued, "We're going to make this a game. You're not donating blood any more. You're going through a portal to another dimension." Kyle ran his finger along the golden gate.

Luka shivered. "What?" Ridiculous. He wasn't a kid anymore.

"Come on, you've got to really *listen*."—he pointed to the hospital—"is the end of your quest. It's really not that bad, you know. It's the journey that is worth living . . . and this one just might kill you."

Kyle had lost it.

"This is ridiculous," said Luka. "I've grown out of games like that. There are no portals. It's all just make-believe." Luka *hated* make-believe.

"Oh, and one more thing," Kyle continued. "You're going to send that application."

"What application?" Luka tried not to react. Had Kyle gone through his things?

"You know." Kyle smirked.

And then he disappeared.

Luka's heart felt like it was going to rip itself out of his chest. He stepped forward and peered through the gate. Everything looked normal. The lush, green lawn they'd played on as kids still sloped down to the duck pond and gazebos. The path still wound its way up the hill to the bustling main building and the east deck. Of course it seemed normal. It *was* normal.

But there was no sign of Kyle. Where was he? Luka paused. Other questions bothered him, too. How could his brother have known about the application? He hadn't even been home when Luka filled it out. And since when had he been wearing that scarf?

Luka figured he was either going crazy, or it was all some stupid joke. Or—magic. He rolled his eyes. *There's no such thing as magic,* he reminded himself again.

"Okay, very funny," shouted Luka. He glanced around him. People were giving him strange looks and moving slowly away from him. "You've got me. You can come out now." Luka removed an earbud and strained to hear Kyle's hoarse chuckle. It didn't come.

Behind him, the hum of the coffee machine in the food truck stopped. Hushed voices swirled around him as he swayed. Someone in scrubs reached for him.

"Are you okay?" the blurry face asked.

Luka backed away, replacing the bud in his ear. He stumbled, steadying himself on the gate. "You're an idiot, you know," he shouted to the empty garden.

Silence answered.

"Okay, fine. I'm listening. *Really* listening," Luka couldn't hide the sarcasm. He rolled his eyes, took a deep breath, and walked through the "portal."

"Luka stumbled through the wormhole and leaned against the open gate, flakes of gold clinging to his sweaty palms," said Kyle. He was sitting in the grass, his legs outstretched.

"Why the hell are you narrating my movements? And how did I not see you there? And . . ." Luka glanced at his hands. What looked like gold leaf was stuck to his damp palms in patches. He scrubbed his hands on his jeans, and the flakes fell to the ground.

Kyle continued, "Behind him, the city skyline shimmered in a hazy blur, like asphalt on a summer's day. People passed by in huddles, earbuds in and noses down, unfazed by the slaughterhouse before them."

Luka's breath was shallow. "This is getting out of . . ."

He glanced back toward Locke's Lane. The gate had been replaced by a shifting rainbow glaze. He touched the portal, which clung to his skin like liquid. It was as though they were trapped within a giant bubble. Everything Kyle had said appeared to be true.

He pinched himself. A slight twinge of pain rippled across his skin.

The reasonable explanation was that Luka had gone mad. Writing that application had made him crack. He probably wouldn't walk in those doors now—no, he'd be going in a straightjacket instead, buckled to a stretcher.

"Oh, don't be so dramatic," said Kyle, jumping to his feet—which, Luka realized, were in clown shoes. "Come on, Scrooge. We're playing a game, that's all. Remember those?"

"What's with those?" Luka asked, looking at his feet.

"*That's* what you're worried about?" Kyle motioned to their surroundings. "Look around. You have other things to worry about. Just check out those clouds."

Shadows gathered overhead, the sky swirling with the threat of a storm. A small halo of light had formed above the hospital, no doubt luring him into the eye. On either side of the path, dull grass shivered in the cold wind.

The path itself was a combination of asymmetrical pavers and gravel where the mortar had washed away over time. Luka had always thought it made his footsteps sound like popping bubblegum. Kyle was up ahead, wobbling on one foot. He looked ridiculous. Suddenly, he hopped onto the other foot, waving his arms wildly as he tried to regain his balance.

Luka realized what he was doing. It had been a while since they'd played The Floor is Lava on this path. Every kid did it, sick or otherwise, but the stakes had been unusually high for them: touch the cracks, and you'd die. It had seemed normal to casually die in games when they were younger. Luka felt a bit uneasy thinking back on it now, but he supposed it wasn't too different from video games. As he gazed up at the brewing storm above, Luka couldn't help but imagine giant, red letters looming in the gray sky.

K.O.

A rumbling began in the distance, and for a moment, Luka assumed it was thunder. But soon the ground began to shake and heave, and the pavers stretched and moved apart. Gravel bounced and fell into a steadily forming chasm below, as did large chunks of the remaining mortar. Lava surged and boiled beneath the path, extreme heat radiating toward them. Kyle stumbled forward, his floppy shoes awkward and inappropriate for the game.

Left and right, left spin and right. Luka had always been considerably more nimble than Kyle, and he knew how to use his hypermobility to his advantage. "You're too bendy," Kyle would say as he bounced awkwardly to and fro, his lanky yet broad frame resembling more of a gorilla than an older brother.

Left and right, leap, tuck, and pivot. Luka caught up to his brother, then raced ahead. He imagined his feet were on tiny springs as he darted back and forth.

When he reached the end of the path and shook his hands in victory, Luka bowed theatrically the way Kyle had earlier. "I got you . . . !"

Luka stopped. Two ridiculous clown shoes lay motionless on the path. Lightning cracked overhead and the sky filled with pure, white light. Eight pale knuckles shone from the edge of the paver, then four, then two. Then none.

"Kyle!"

Luka ran toward him, but it was too late. Kyle fell into the oozing depths below. The pavers shifted back together, the chasm fading into memory. Luka knelt on the edge of the path, clawing at the moist soil. Kyle was gone.

"No, I'm not," said Kyle.

"What the actual fuck?" What game *was* this?

Kyle stood on the deck, leaning against a lamppost. He now wore a tuxedo and a pair of flip-flops. "We meet our brave young hero on the decks of—"

Luka charged at his brother and grabbed him by the collar. "What the actual hell is going on? Tell me now. Am I losing my bloody mind, or . . . or . . . or . . ."

Luka struggled to get both the air in and the words out. What was happening to him? He pushed and shoved as Kyle tried to pin his arms behind him.

"Calm down," said Kyle, which only made him more annoyed.

The boys scuffled along the edge of the deck until Kyle lost his footing. Luka was still holding onto him when they fell into a lavender bush. Still wrestling, they kept rolling, tumbling down the soft, grassy hill until they came to a stop by the duck pond.

"Wow." Kyle was already back on his feet. "Haven't done that in a while. Good idea!"

Luka started to speak, but he couldn't find the words. Instead, he gazed at the hill as though struck by a bolt of lightning—or a memory. When they were younger, he and his brother would roll down the hill endlessly while their father sipped lemonade and their mother worried about the various injuries they never ended up getting.

"What is all this?" Luka asked quietly.

"I told you." Kyle chuckled. "Games. We used to do this all the time before . . . everything. Life, I suppose."

Luka sighed. "You don't get it, do you?"

"What?"

"I don't have time for games. *You* don't have time for games. This stuff is serious, and it's real. I should be in there right now." Luka heaved, his lungs straining for air.

"Yeah, but you hate it in there. I'm trying to help."

"You can't help. There are some things I have to do on my own." Luka's eyes dropped. "You weren't in there all the time like I was. You didn't lose weeks, months, of your life. All the tests, all the treatment . . . You don't know what it's like to never know if it's going to come back." Luka crossed his legs and sighed.

"Yes, I do." Kyle sat beside him and removed his notebook from the pocket of his tuxedo. He flicked through the pages. There were pictures of the two of them skating, swimming, laughing. In one, Luka was an astronaut. In another, he wore a cape as he rescued a cat from a tree.

"I was there with you every weekend." Kyle's head drooped low. "I saw what you went through. We all did. I read to you when you were spaced out for days. I gave you the bucket when you puked. I hugged you when you cried. Honestly, I felt useless. I wanted to help you so bad, but I couldn't figure out how."

Kyle paused at a picture of them on a rollercoaster. Together.

"I . . ." Luka's voice was barely a whisper. He hadn't thought of it that way.

"I know."

. . .

The pond rippled as the first few drops of rain struck its surface.

"Come on," said Luka, offering his hand to his brother, who took it with a smile.

The clouds had an eerie green tinge and they hung low above the hospital, as if the boys could touch them if they stretched far enough. A drop of acid rain fell on Luka's shoulder and sizzled through his hoodie, singeing his skin.

Kyle inspected the mock injury, cracking half a smile before he sprinted off toward the hospital with Luka close behind. By the time they made it up the hill, their tattered clothes hung loosely from their scarred flesh. Sneaking under the cover of the deck, through the doors of the east entrance, and into a side hallway, the boys made their way to the restroom, laughing.

Luka didn't know what to think. His clothes were back to normal, although they were damp, so the rain must have been real. Staring into the mirror, Luka tugged his hoodie down below his collarbone and traced the smooth scar where his chemotherapy port had been implanted beneath his skin. Friends had suggested covering it with a tattoo, but that didn't feel quite right to him.

The toilet flushed, and Kyle joined him at the sinks. He was dressed in a doctor's coat and scrubs, a stethoscope hanging around his neck. "So, this deal . . ." he started. "I'm helping you, just like I said. But I need you to help me, too. You need to understand . . ."

Luka stared. His heart raced, and he was itching to

continue. "Why do your outfits keep changing? Did you steal that from somewhere? They're going to know."

"Man, you really don't pay much attention, do you?" Kyle dried his hands and opened the door. "Come on, let's go find those bloodsuckers."

Kyle made his way through the crowded atrium toward the information desk. The woman behind the counter stared directly at Luka. Maybe he had looked a bit crazy sprinting into the hospital moments earlier. She seemed oblivious to Kyle, who slipped behind her and glanced at some paperwork. Luka wondered how he was getting away with it unnoticed.

A firm hand landed on Luka's shoulder. The man with the blurry face wore a security guard's uniform, and his other hand was curled around his baton. He said something Luka couldn't make out.

"Cops and robbers!" Luka's shout echoed through the atrium. "Good one, Kyle."

"Don't touch him." Suddenly, Kyle stood between them, knocking the guard's arm away.

Luka backed away, smirking.

The guard stared straight at Kyle, but he seemed confused. He, too, appeared to look right through him. Kyle shrugged.

The woman behind the counter was ushering people away. Luka's imagination—or their acting—was unbelievably real. They almost looked scared of . . . him? Ridiculous. Luka always played the role of the cop, and Kyle was usually the robber.

The guard's eyes fixed on Luka again, and he grabbed him by the shoulder, hard.

"Ouch!" said Luka. Since when had these games hurt?

Luka spun, twisting his arm in its socket—thankful once more for his overly flexible joints—as he shuffled past the guard into the startled crowd. People backed away from him as small gasps and shrieks filled the room. The guard rushed toward him, but Luka darted around a corner and up a staircase, patients and visitors jumping back in surprise.

Kyle was nowhere to be seen.

The guard called something into a walkie-talkie, but Luka was certain he knew the hospital better than him. They were always rehiring, and he doubted the man had much experience wandering these halls. Luka, on the other hand, was long overdue for his service, and where he wanted to go was nowhere near a guard's room.

Luka dashed through corridors, past the cafeteria, and up a second set of stairs. At first, the guard followed closely, but soon the distance between them grew. The guard's legs tired, while Luka's pace matched the rate of his heart. He sprinted through a skyway into the north wing of the hospital. When the coast was clear, he slipped into an empty room and locked himself in the bathroom, panting.

Kyle was already there.

Luka jumped. "Where did you come from?"

"Yeah, about that." Kyle pushed a pair of yellow glasses up on the bridge of his nose. Where *did* he keep getting all these stupid accessories?

Luka opened the door an inch and peered through. From this angle, he had a narrow view of the hallway. Nurses went about their routines while a food cart hummed down the hall. The cart stopped, and a lunch lady slid a tray out and entered another room. No signs of security.

Luka closed the door and faced Kyle. "Well?" he whispered.

"So, I think . . . I'm . . . like . . . not really here?" Kyle started.

What kind of game was this?

"I don't know if I'm me or if I'm you, in your head or . . ."

Luka stumbled against the sink. "You're crazy."

"Think about it."

Luka had imagined lava and portals and acid rain. Perhaps he'd imagined his brother, too. It would explain the stupid outfits, not to mention why everyone looked through him. "So . . ." Luka wiped his brow. "I *am* crazy, then."

"I'm not sure." Kyle slumped onto a stool in the shower.

Outside, the hum of the cart began, then faded into the distance.

"All I know is"—Kyle shrugged—"I had to help you get here."

"So you're me, helping me get here. Gee, thanks. Maybe you should help me get into the psych ward." Luka reached into his pocket, pulling out Kyle's notebook and pen. He must have had them all along. A lump formed in his throat. How many people had seen him acting like that? His face paled.

"At least it means the real me doesn't know about your college application, right?" Kyle chuckled.

Luka laughed. "Yeah, I guess so."

"Why don't you want me knowing about it anyway?"

"I don't know. I guess I don't really put myself out there anymore."

"That's not it." Kyle crossed his legs impatiently.

"All right then, *me*. If *I* am so smart, why am I so scared?"

Kyle sighed. "You're scared you'll get sick again."

Luka closed his eyes.

"And look, you might. But what's the point? You're going to let life pass you by because you're afraid of living."

The room fell silent. Kyle was gone.

. . .

Luka removed his hoodie and set it on the sink. He stared into his reflection as if expecting Kyle to detach himself and wander out of it. In a weird way, he felt like he was truly seeing himself for the first time in . . . forever.

Kyle—or Luka himself—had said he didn't really listen. He also didn't really look. Or feel. Or live. He had also said that three lives could be saved. Whose lives? Why wasn't the *real* Kyle here with him? Luka felt like there was still something he wasn't really *seeing*.

Luka made his way out of the bathroom and into the empty room. There were no signs of security guards, no acid, no lava . . . but also no Kyle. At this point, he had no clue which parts of the day were real. In the hallway, staff, patients, and visitors all came and went. Luckily, no one seemed bothered by—or scared of—his presence.

As he walked through the ward toward the main corridor, he realized where he was. *Cancer and Wellness.* Some doors were open. He glimpsed faces of varying ages. He saw in them the same things he felt: happiness, laughter, sadness, pain. Luka gulped. Even though he knew he was missing something, he knew what he had to do.

Three measly pints.

Three lives.

Three *specific* lives that had always been there for him.

The kitchenette in the pathology department was painted in an eerie shade of dark red. A peculiar choice, even for bloodsuckers, Luka thought. Even though he felt sad that his brother wasn't with him, Luka was glad they'd never played Vampires in real life.

The donation was surprisingly uneventful. He drank a ton of water and filled out a questionnaire, got his finger pricked to test his blood, and then relaxed in a recliner while the nurse took his blood. Three measly pints.

After a few minutes, he made his way into the kitchenette and sat down to people watch. Most had their eyes fixed on the television as it played reruns of the morning news. A car had flipped on the highway outside of town. Luka looked away.

A couple were discussing a woman named Sandy and how she couldn't possibly justify that new purse because of the way her husband's job was going, but then, that was Sandy: head in the sand and eyes on the prize. Luka snickered to himself as he thought of his brother. If only Kyle were here to hear this.

He unfolded his hoodie on his lap and reached into the pocket. Kyle's notebook was wet and a little bit crumpled. Luka flicked through the book, smoothing out the pages as he went. The book was filled with excerpts of conversations, drawings of the two of them, jokes or random words Kyle thought were funny. *Superfluous. Meldrop. Biblioklept.*

Luka found a page titled "101 Things to do with Scrooge after College.' Luka wasn't fond of the nickname, but it had been fairly accurate. At the end of the list, he added, "Play more games."

After a while, a different nurse approached.

"Mr. Hawthorne?" she asked.

"It's just Luka."

"Luka," she repeated, "your parents and your brother are in recovery. Your donation today has been incredibly helpful. It was a terrible crash, but they're going to be okay."

"Thank you." Luka stared blankly at the nurse. On the outside, he could have been a statue. On the inside, he thought he might implode. A million thoughts swelled against his ears and pulsed in his veins. Three specific lives. "Can I go see them?"

"Yes, but take it easy."

Luka flew out of the chair, his head fuzzy and his body wobbly.

"Here." The nurse shoved another sandwich and some Jell-O into his hand, the hoodie and notebook still crammed into the other. She smiled at him as he left, half-running toward the door.

As he rushed through the corridors toward his family, Luka ran through the wave of thoughts and emotions that flooded his brain. He was going crazy. No doubt about it. There was no such thing as magic or portals. There had been no lava or acid rain. His brother hadn't played childish games with him on the way to the hospital.

Even so, Luka felt relieved, mostly because his family was okay, but also because he'd decided to start living. And first thing Monday, he would mail that college application.

He'd probably still keep his bed neat and tidy, though. And there wasn't anything wrong with getting to places a minute early.

Luka sighed with relief as he reached Recovery. His parents weren't out yet, but Kyle was in a room down the hall. All three were doing well.

Kyle lay sleeping in a room overlooking the hospital grounds. Luka tiptoed in and stood by the window. Outside, the rain kept pouring, splashing against the third floor gutter. The kidney-shaped pond below rippled and surged with the down-pour, and the grass looked heavy and sodden. A few scattered umbrellas made their way down the path toward the empty coffee van in Locke's Lane.

His brother was covered in bruises and bandages. The wall behind him kept up a slow and steady beat of beeps. Kyle twitched, and Luka wondered if he was dreaming. Even though the magic hadn't been real, this Kyle definitely was.

He stepped toward him and stumbled into something light. A large cardboard box lay on the floor by his brother's bed. In thick black marker were the words, "Costumes and Accessories."

Luka reached into the box and pulled out a purple satin top hat. Below it were a number of unusual items. Yellow glasses. A green scarf. Polka-dot clown shoes. A doctor's coat and a stethoscope . . .

Luka's face paled. "There's no such thing as magic," he whispered.

Kyle opened his eyes and chuckled.

About the Author

Victoria Young is a Brit-born, Aussie-grown new author who's desk overlooks ghostly gums and a duck-filled kiddie pool. When she's not writing, she runs a small business with her husband and enjoys toddler wrangling, painting and gardening. She's currently trying to Tetris her small suburban farm to include more fruit trees. There's around sixty.

Justin the Just

JAY TEA MORIARTY

On a dark night, past midnight, the rain-slicked city streets were crowded with cheap men and desperate deals. Justin stalked between shadows toward the Last Alley Bar. His eyes flickered feral yellow, his neat, greedy teeth hidden under a wide-brimmed hat and unkempt hair.

His target was a drunk man lumbering out the back of the bar on wobbly legs. The man retched in the gutter before wiping his mouth. He shook his head to clear it, then noticed someone watching him.

"Ah, 'ullo there, frien'," he slurred. "How're ya doin'?"

"I do fine this merry night, *friend*," Justin replied in a honey-sweet voice. Anyone who knew him would recognize it as his business voice.

The drunk leered up at him. "Friend, huh? I ain't your frien', though you do look a likely sort. Lemme get a lookachya." The drunk man shook himself again and used the wet fencing to right himself. The light still hid Justin's face. "'Ere, I can't see you."

"Allow me," Justin said, and stepped into the light. The

illumination from an upstairs window highlighted the scar that ran from cheek to ear and his wicked devil's tick of a smile. "Friend I said, and friend I meant."

The drunk froze. "You ain't no frien'. You're a demon!"

Justin's tone was warm. "A demon with a gun, yes, and a devil with a knife. But no, my parents were both human, I assure you." With practiced smoothness, Justin drew back his coat, displaying the pistol in its holster. "Your choice. Whether warm or cold, I collect, friend."

The drunk immediately sobered up, his eyes showing panic. Who hadn't heard of Justin the Just? He wasn't just in his methods; rather, he would catch you *just* because there was a bounty on your head. He didn't care who paid or how much, and he always collected.

The drunk tried a different tactic. "Come now, friend, have a heart." He stumbled forward. "Turn me in warm, and I'm dead on the doorstep you deliver me to. Cold, and I'm just a heavy carcass for you to lug about." He tried a winning smile, but he looked like a dog about to bite.

Justin shrugged, considering. "Not much of a difference to me. I can lug a man twice your size without much effort." Justin's tone softened. "Interesting use of the term 'friend,' as though you're aligning yourself with me. Tell you what, take my gun." He drew the pistol and spun the grip toward the man. "You can walk with me to the dropoff, then do yourself in. That way, I haven't turned you in alive, and you haven't forced me to carry you." He smiled warmly, dimples appearing in his stubble. In this lighting, the demon was gone and he was simply Justin.

The drunk gave him a feral grin. "Death to you, and a curse on your friendship!" Grabbing the gun, he fired point blank at Justin's face.

Justin stood still, waiting for the drunk's triumphant smile to fade. It happened gradually as the man realized that the gun had clicked when the hammer hit, but there was no explosion or recoil, just a telling smile on Justin's face.

"Some friend you turned out to be." Justin laughed. He stepped inside the man's reach with one fluid movement, retrieved and loaded the pistol, and fired behind himself to claim his reward.

The few windows up and down the back alley that displayed curious silhouettes were suddenly vacated. The show was over. Another deal in blood, taken by Justin the Just.

Two days later, Justin walked into the Broken Glass Bar and took his usual seat. The Broken Glass was an upper city dive where shadows were the norm and the air smelled of hidden figures and stale smoke. The music was surprisingly light, as though the owner thought pop chart hits were the perfect cover for hired killers working in broad daylight.

Justin's booth had a blue lampshade with a broken light bulb. At first Sam, the bartender, had kept changing it, but when no bulb stayed unbroken for longer than two straight days, he realized who was breaking them and left the booth alone.

Sam watched as Justin entered. Today, a massive figure in a white suite already sat in the bounty hunter's booth. This caused Justin to pause for a split second. Anybody else watching would not have seen it, but the bartender knew how Justin moved and noted the odd angle of his shoe, not even ten degrees off.

"The usual?" Sam called out.

Justin got to his booth and sat down, ignoring the question. "Pleased to finally meet you," he said, waving away the bowl of olives the other man offered him. "No thanks. I'm watching my figure."

The man in white shrugged and pulled the olives back. "Suit yourself. Call me Mr. Krank. You've completed your job." It was a statement, not a question.

"And you've paid me." Justin swallowed, agitated by having someone else in his booth.

Mr. Krank nodded, chewing around an olive and spitting out the pit. "With extra for the warm delivery. How did you manage that?" He sucked his teeth, mildly impressed.

Justin had shot the drunk through the lung and shoulder, enough to incapacitate him but not him kill him immediately. "Reverse psychology. And looking dumber than I am always helps. I handed him the gun and told him to shoot himself. When he naturally turned the gun on me and heard the empty click, the fear was overwhelming. People really wet themselves when they know they've tipped their hand."

Mr. Krank nodded. "My agents saw the events unfold. They occurred as you describe them. How would you like another job?"

"I'll want triple for it," Justin replied. "The last target was far too easy for the price you paid. Therefore, I assume you were testing *me*."

"You're a very astute young man." Mr. Krank leaned forward, and weak light stretched across the room to illuminate his wide, toothy smile. "Had we not known you were the one to apprehend our drunken friend, we never would have guessed it was your work—very clean. How do you do it? Who taught you?"

Justin shrugged. "I deal in blood, not information."

"Please, please," pressed Mr. Krank, his mouth puckering as he lit a fat cigar. "One answer at a time. Yes, we wanted to see your skills. And yes, our next target is harder—much harder." He snapped his fingers impatiently, and a shadowy figure appeared out of the bar's shadows, placing a manila folder on the table before Justin. "Everything you need is in the folder, including your pay in advance. We have provided extra to cover any equipment required. Do you accept?"

Justin didn't move. He was getting edgy waiting for this crank to vacate his booth. He couldn't think. He needed a drink, preferably water. Ice cold. Something that numbed the tongue and provided a brief, mind-sharpening brain freeze if drunk fast enough. Then he could figure everything out. "Yes, of course," he blurted out.

Across the way, the bartender snorted a warning. Justin couldn't tell whether it was for him or not.

"Are you sure, *friend?*" asked the client, deliberately exhaling a huge plume of cigar smoke into Justin's face. The thick, slate-blue cloud hung between them, an imp's tickle in the air.

Justin's eyes stung and his skin felt dirty. He was going mad. "I'm sure, I'm sure!" He scowled and put his hand on the table firmly. "Now get out." There was a heavy clunk on the table as Justin's other hand came up, holding his gun. "I need to meditate on this."

The shadowy figure moved forward, but was stayed by Mr. Krank. "Allow our friend room for his aggression," he said casually. "We have been indulging in uncouth behavior. I bid you a good day, Justin."

Bowing and wiping his mouth on a napkin, Mr. Krank rose and waved a hand. All the other people in the bar got up, and after one of them checked that the exit was clear, they followed the dark figure of Mr. Krank out of the Broken Glass.

Justin watched, amazed, as the place cleared out. "Are you having a laugh?" he couldn't help but ask.

The boss didn't respond as he left, but the light by the door was just enough to make out his face. A grizzled, well-worn frown. Dark eyebrows like bushy caterpillars. A scar terrible as red lightning, rising all the way from the left lip to above the left eye. Who was this madman, this Mr. Krank?

Left alone, Justin could finally breathe. After the full, noisy room, the silence was deafening. "Who was that?" Justin asked the bartender.

"You didn't hear my warning, didja, kid?" The bartender tossed a bottle of vodka to Justin, and he caught it. "On the house. Look inside the folder."

"But I don't drink," Justin said, pushing the bottle aside and pulling the manilla folder toward him. He flipped it open and read the page before him—or would have, if his concentration hadn't shattered. He saw his own face on the papers before him. The document read, "Open contract. First to submit target to be paid one million dollars."

"Hey," he said weakly, "what is this...?" He looked at the bartender, who pointed at the bottle of vodka again.

"Thanks," Justin said, shaking. He stood up on rubbery legs before snatching up the bottle and leaving the barroom amid a scattering of pages that mirrored his state of mind.

In the bathroom, he turned on the water and wet his face. Looking up, he saw the lank blond hair over his eyes and the scar on his left cheek, a ragged line running to his ear. "Do I run? Where can I hide?"

Power was one thing and corruption another, but controlling whole rooms filled with thugs? Paying assassins to hit themselves? This Krank had to be a madman, and he played brilliant mind games.

His father's words came to him. "You ever scared boy, you face it. You turn and set yer feet, and if it's somethin' you can't beat, you'll know it right away. Not later, not after a life o' fear."

"Right away," Justin repeated. "Right *now*." And for a

moment, he saw his father's face in the mirror, not his own. Father winked, drawing a line across his throat.

Justin winked back, grabbed the bottle of vodka, and left the bathroom.

"Where ya going?" Sam called out.

Justin heard nothing. He stepped out the door into the enclosed stairwell that led down to the street, and shouted in a clear voice, "Hey, Mr. Krank! Are you ready to die?"

The bartender closed the front door and locked it, throwing away the key. Then he hid in the bathroom with the light off.

He still didn't feel any safer.

"What is that pup yelling about?" asked Mr. Krank, turning around at the sound of Justin's voice. The mobster and his gang of thirty men and women had gathered at the bottom of the stairs, about to enter the street. They had been smoking and joking with one another when Justin's shout came down the stairway. "You two, go and see what's happened. He can't have cracked already."

The stairs were made up of three flights that crisscrossed back and forth several times, forming a tall, repeating Z pattern all the way up. This was all housed within the building itself, originally intended as a fire escape but now used as a back entrance to the Broken Glass.

Two men at the back of the group peeled off, heading up the stairs with guns drawn. They had just disappeared around the first bend when there was gunfire, and then silence.

"Shit! He can't be down the stairs already . . . *can he?*" When no response came, Mr. Krank grabbed the closest thug, a brunette with cruel eyes. "Go and take a look. Did they shoot the goddamn cleaning lady?"

"Good one, boss," laughed the woman, drawing her gun

and making her way up the first flight. Something clear and oblong came flying down the stairs. A vodka bottle connected with her head, knocking her out.

Murmurs came from the gangsters before they took a collective step toward the door leading out into the street. In a rustle of cloth, Justin the Just leaped over the top railing, his black trench coat billowing in the air. There were gasps and yelps as the thugs spread out, but not before Justin fired three neat shots with a dead-steady arm. In the ensuing confusion, he landed on his feet and rolled to safety.

Three of the gangsters collapsed to the ground as the rest drew their guns and returned fire. Bullets riddled the staircase and walls. The sudden appearance of the legendary marksman and the loss of their own numbers had the effect Justin wanted. So many people were shooting in panic that friendly fire killed another five hired hands.

"Stop, you idiots!" shouted Mr. Krank, smacking those closest to him with a beringed fist. "He wants you to shoot each other!"

The shooting stopped.

"So what do we do, boss? It's Justin the Just!"

"I know that! Did you not read the file on him, you putz? I've put a million dollar contract on his head."

The remaining twenty thugs, now recalling the bounty, all smiled greedily. "Timone, you got that grenade?" asked one.

Timone, a short man with a powerful throwing arm, stepped forward. He squinted. "Indeed, I do. Cover me."

Guns were trained on Justin's last known position as Timone crept forward. He carefully timed the explosive. Careful to lob the grenade upward so it would explode on the flight above, he counted aloud. "Five, four, three—"

Movement came from under the stairwell, a flash of blond hair and a black trench coat, before Justin's gun barked and a single bullet ripped into Timone's fist. The grenade exploded, taking out the thugs in the immediate vicinity. Timone was beside himself. Timone was beside everyone.

The bottom landing of the stairs had splintered, scorch marks and debris covering the floor. As the dust cleared and shrapnel rained down, the boss spluttered, "Q-quick, now's our chance! Everyone, pile into the staircase! He can't take us all out! *Two million* to whoever brings me his head!"

Anger and greed stirred in the gangsters' hearts, only thirteen strong now but enraged enough to equal the strength of their lost comrades. One brave individual took point, peeking around the doorframe before waving everyone else in.

"I don't see him," said a blonde with red contact lenses.

"Perhaps he went back up the stairs?" suggested a man with a split eyebrow.

"I'll cover you," said the thug on point, aiming his gun upward as the rest began climbing again. As they ascended, he motioned for the boss, who joined them as they filed up the stairs.

"Do you see him now?" asked Mr. Krank, feeling jittery.

"Nothing," called a female voice. "The bar is closed, and the door is locked. I can call out for Sam."

"You leave that bartender alone," Mr. Krank growled back. "He's been good business for everyone. We won't get him involved."

"So ... how do we find Justin?" asked someone.

"How should I know?" another replied.

"Actually," said a crisp, clean voice, like the first star of the night, "I think Sam has done terribly by you guys."

Everyone turned toward the voice. Behind them stood a tall figure with a blond shock of hair, a black trench coat, and a gun in one hand. Beside him was the brave—but now unconscious—thug, a black eye already developing.

Justin smiled. His gun was aimed casually at Mr. Krank's back, while his other hand held the bottle of vodka. He had recovered it after finding it near the body of the brunette he had knocked out earlier. "I mean, Sam didn't tell you just how good I am, did he?"

Mr. Krank turned his head to look over his shoulder. "You think you're smart because you can duck around us all, boy?" he snarled.

"Smart has nothing to do with it," Justin said, now raising the gun level with Mr. Krank's head. Every thug on the first flight of stairs trained their weapons on him. "Uh-uh! You shoot me, and I am definitely quick enough to shoot Mr. Boss here. Who's gonna pay you then?"

A shot went off, winging Justin in the shoulder. Gritting his teeth bitterly, Justin aimed lower and fired.

A slug hit Mr. Krank in the foot. He screamed and dropped to one knee. "Shit!"

"I just shot your boss in the pinky toe. That's your only warning. You can stay to fight it out and I'll add you to my kill count, or you can leave and I won't pursue you . . . today."

The gangsters laughed. Despite the generous offer, no one left. Justin thought he heard footsteps farther up, but he couldn't be sure.

"So what now?" said Mr. Krank. "We're at a stalemate, Justin. If they shoot you and you shoot me, then we're all dead. On the other hand, if you shoot me first, they'll gun you down, and once again we're all dead and no one gets the money. How about we strike a bargain?"

Justin smiled, drawing circles with his gun muzzle. "You'd like that very much, wouldn't you? Negotiating so soon looks like weakness, if you ask me."

"You have me at a disadvantage. What are my options?"

The boss raised his eyebrows, feigning nonchalance. "We can both end the day alive and rich."

Justin looked around the staircase, then up it, and came to a conclusion. "I'm going to shoot you," he said, "although it's not fair to these poor people you've employed. I feel like they should be given a chance."

A curious voice spoke from above. "What do you mean by not fair?"

Justin looked up but couldn't identify the speaker. "I've already taken out half your crew and shot your boss's toe off, all while taking only a slight graze to the shoulder. Do you really feel confident? You don't think I can take out Mr. Krank here—and most of you—before *one* of you gets close enough for a shot?"

This time Justin heard voices mumbling about the odds, and he liked the sound of that. Feet shuffled above as the gangsters either left or gathered closer together for the final showdown. The devil within him took in a deep, dark breath.

"Here's what I'm going to do," he started. "I'm going to shoot your boss, then fire at all of you as I backpedal out the door and into the street. If you follow me, you won't like it. If you head on up the stairs and stay there until you count to one thousand, I'll leave you alone. For the rest of today, anyway."

"Bullshit!" yelled a man. "You can't take all of us."

"I've done perfectly fine so far."

"You think you're a hero?" shouted a man in the front.

"Yeah, aren't you scared?" jeered another.

"Me? I'm terrified," answered Justin honestly. "Any stray shot could pierce my heart. But at least this way, I know I'm taking you with me, and I might even get out unscathed."

"Enough of this pissing and moaning!" Mr. Krank growled. He turned, sure and powerful, swinging a fist the size of a bowling ball at Justin. The bounty hunter was spry enough to hop backward, dropping and turning it into a roll before coming up onto his legs. Being this close to the boss was all Justin needed.

Mr. Krank grunted angrily but stepped in quick again with another heavy swing. Justin danced back, sweeping out his coat, using the boss as a human shield. None of the thugs fired. Dodging another fist, then a wide leg sweep, Justin opened the bottle of vodka.

"Time to fly!" Justin sang out, and fired his weapon point blank into Mr. Krank's leg. The shin fractured and splintered inward, dropping the large man. "You can die with them," Justin spat before he fired two more shots at the stairwell—not at the thugs, who immediately returned fire, but at the balusters.

Splinters and wood chips sprayed everywhere. The precise shots, coupled with the grenade damage, caused the first flight of stairs to lose structural integrity. It came crashing down. Thugs fell backward, shielding their eyes as Justin emptied a clip and dashed outside.

He fled into the street, ejecting the empty magazine and jamming his gun into a pocket, where a fresh clip clicked easily into place. Hastily, he pulled out a bandana and held it in his mouth before fumbling with a lighter and the bottle of vodka.

"Come back here, you bastard!" Mr. Krank groaned, tears in his eyes as he rolled around in anger and pain.

Justin took two steps before a hard metal slug zinged past his sleeve. He turned and saw the doorway filled with gangsters. One stood on either side of the door while others popped into view to scope out his location. And there he was in plain view, out in the middle of the street fumbling with a red hanky.

"Give up!" a thug shouted. "You're out in the open. Admit it, *you're cooked!*"

Justin, wearing the smile he'd practiced for when he met

the devil, just laughed. "When you get to hell, tell Timone *not* to count out loud for me."

He threw the molotov cocktail. Every set of eyes opened wide with fear. The thugs screamed and scrambled to get out of the way. Justin watched it all. The bottle spun once before landing in the stairwell, filling the area with flames and smoke that belched out the door. Two men managed to escape, and Justin put each of them down with a clean shot through the lungs.

The vengeful flames took hold of the building and began to creep up its many levels. The screams of terrified gangsters mingled with the crackling flames as Justin the Just turned on his heel.

"I feel better now," he said to the world at large. "All I wanted was my damn booth back."

*

Sam the bartender sat across from Justin, a tense look on his face. Since Sam's place had mysteriously burned down, they were in the White Brick, a seedy bar across town. Justin knew Sam didn't mind too much. Given his clientele, the Broken Glass had definitely been insured.

Sam had a briefcase with him, which he now pushed across the table to Justin. "It's all there, every cent. He really did put a million dollars on your head."

Justin took the briefcase and patted it without looking inside. "Yeah, I know. Thank God the advance was in cash." Justin drummed his fingers, then stood up. "He almost had me rattled. Thanks for the vodka."

. . .

*

It was another day. Another client. Another life. Someone had a big target, and had heard that Justin the Just dealt in big blood these days.

"Yes, I deal in big blood. But I charge a big dollars, too."

The client, who looked like a bull on steroids, grunted, unimpressed. "So what, you're the new boss? I'm not impressed. Don't you have some corny catchphrase like, 'I'll deliver the meat, cold or warm'? How is that professional?"

"It's simple," Justin said, affording the client a winning smile. "Cold or warm means dead or alive. You should ask Mr. Olive about it some time."

"Who's Mr. Olive?"

"Sorry, a personal joke of mine. I meant Mr. Krank."

The client went silent. Too silent. "I heard about that. Did you say the same thing to him?"

Justin shook his head regretfully. "Unfortunately not, but I did have a good one planned for him. He was going to be *well done*."

The client whistled. "And they say he came after *you?* What an idiot."

Justin winked.

About the Author

Jay Tea Moriarty writes Science Fiction. His series, *The Full Life of a Robot* explores deep topics like being human, or as close as possible without the actual tag. By placing a robot in human situations, at what point does the empathy of a human evaporate and why?

Moriarty also writes Fantasy often asking wholesome questions that could cost the characters all they have.

If a character puts everything on the line, they can look death in the face, and with a plan and the right companions at their side, they have a chance to survive.

To earn his daily bread, Moriarty has given up being a shill seller of lottery tickets, instead looking after his new spawn while writing. That is, attempting to write. One of his cat helpers has since joined the great yarn factory in the sky, but he's adopted another loveable kitty, who is also no help writing whatsoever.

facebook.com/Jtmoriartywriter

twitter.com/jtmoriartywriter

instagram.com/jtmoriartywriter

bookbub.com/authors/j-t-moriarty

amazon.com/stores/Jay-Tea-Moriarty/author/B0B3N7FD76

Acknowledgments

With every anthology that we have published, loads of work goes on behind the scenes. So there are quite a few people to thank.

First and foremost, each and every writer involved. Deals in Blood is the forth anthology in four years and in that time, it has been so exciting to see the growth of these writers, be part of their writing process, and have developed a supportive community for many anthologies to come.

These writers have full lives, living adventures, family responsibilities, and careers to keep up with. But creative people must create. And they took the time to deep dive into their imaginations and create a story that they are passionate about.

Every time I hit the publish button, my heart swells just knowing how magical the process has been. I hope that our love for literature translates into the stories.

Thank you to Amy Elmore for being our amazing editor. J.T. Moriarty for turning up and being the biggest support there is. Victoria Young and Michelle Crow for your honesty. Chris Masterton for the blurb. Bruno Gomes for always stepping up to help right at the last minute. I swear I'm trying not to do that anymore. But you've always have had our backs.

To the readers, thank you for supporting our little community. Your reviews are read and we hear you! Your words of support light all of our hearts.

More Anthologies